GXM731

TERRY RAY

SUNBURY PRESS

Mechanicsburg, Pennsylvania   USA

Published by Sunbury Press, Inc.
50 West Main Street, Suite A
Mechanicsburg, Pennsylvania 17055

www.sunburypress.com

For information about special discounts for bulk purchases, please contact Sunbury Press Orders Dept. at (855) 338-8359 or orders@sunburypress.com.

To request one of our authors for speaking engagements or book signings, please contact Sunbury Press Publicity Dept. at publicity@sunburypress.com.

ISBN: 978-1-62006-330-9 (Trade Paperback)
ISBN: 978-1-62006-331-6 (Mobipocket)
ISBN: 978-1-62006-332-3 (ePub)

FIRST SUNBURY PRESS EDITION: December 2013

Product of the United States of America
0 1 1 2 3 5 8 13 21 34 55

Set in Bookman Old Style
Designed by Lawrence Knorr
Cover by Lawrence Knorr
Edited by Angela Wagner

Continue the Enlightenment!

OTHER BOOKS BY
TERRY RAY

The Crossers Series:

The Man in the Mountain

The Circle

Crossing the Valley

Path to Armageddon

ACKNOWLEDGMENTS

Captain Video, Buck Rogers. *Lost in Space*, Jules Verne, H.G. Wells, *Star Trek*, *Star Wars*, *2001 - A Space Odyssey*, John Glenn, Alan Sheppard, *Science Fiction Theater*, *The Twilight Zone*, *UFO Files*, *Ancient Aliens*, Carl Sagan, MUFON, and my childhood friends - with whom I spent endless summers in a big cardboard box, pretending we were spacemen.

"There are more things in heaven and earth,
Horatio, Than are dreamt of in your philosophy."

Wm. Shakespeare's *Hamlet*

CHAPTER 1

Thanner brought his very hot cup of tea to his nose. It had a very pleasant, fruit-like fragrance. Feeling the heat, he returned the cup to the table for cooling. He looked across the table at his wife. She once again shook her head and looked down into her own cup of tea. Thanner knew he was required to ask – so he did.

"What's the matter, honey?"

She shook her head a third time, then responded.

"I just can't believe they're sending you out again, Thanner. You've only been home for less than a week."

"Yeah ... I know. Apparently I'm indispensable."

"Well ... where are they sending you this time?"

"GXM 731."

"Again?"

"Yep ... again."

"What is with that planet?"

"It's a beautiful little planet ... and it's on the no-contact list ... and it's a little too tempting for some of the sectors. I'm sure you can guess who."

"The Enrues?"

"Not this time."

"The Olenreths?"

"You got it."

"What is the problem those two sectors? They're forever causing trouble."

"You've always got a few who act as though the rules don't apply to them. You'd think they would know better – after we blew the Enrues' main ship out of the air, about a hundred years ago, for an intervention on 731. The Olenreths saw us do it."

"You were on that mission, as I recall."

"Yeah ... I was. It was my second assignment."

"That was a long time ago, sweetheart."

"It was."

1

Thanner fell silent and his eyes became distant. The suddenness of his mood change alarmed Remmy.

"What is it, Thanner?"

Thanner remained quiet and seemed unsure of what to say. He looked at Remmy with plaintive eyes.

"I really didn't think I'd tell you this ... but I guess I'm going to."

"What?"

"Well ... when Enton got killed on this last trip ..." He stopped.

"Yes ..."

"I feel bad saying this."

"What? Saying what?"

"Remmy ... when I saw him lying there – dead ... I envied him."

"Thanner! Why would you say such a thing!?"

"Remmy ... when's the last time you saw a baby?"

"What does that have to do with the discussion?"

"Just humor me. How long has it been?"

"Oh ... whatever, Thanner ... I guess it was about two years ago when I was food shopping. Satisfied?"

"And do you realize that Enton's wife will now get a Replacement Certificate?"

"I actually hadn't thought about that."

"How do you feel about that?"

"Honestly? I'm envious."

"And you're envious because almost no one has babies anymore, right?"

"Yes, Thanner."

"And no one has weddings anymore ... or romance ... or any of those things that made life special when we were growing up. All the things that were the life of the heart are gone now."

"Oh stop with those out-dated literary phrases from all those old novels you're always reading. Yes ... there was young love and all the excitement that went with it – but there was also heartbreak involved in 'the life of the heart' as you are so fond of saying. For me ... no thanks. Before I met you, I had my heart broken – twice – and those were two of the worst experiences of my life. I'd never want to go through it again – or see anyone else go through it, either. And the grief I went through when my dad died ... I thought I'd never get over it. You remember. I spent months lying in bed – crying all the time. I wasn't the same for years. You think I'd wish that on Dansue? He'll never have to go through such pain. And think of all the little children who used to die from disease. Do you really want to go back to that? If Dansue had died when he was a baby, I would have stopped living. I would have killed myself. I really would have. Now, we will always have our son with us. We'll never lose him. I really do think you should stop reading those old novels, Thanner. They just make you unhappy ... then you make me unhappy ... so what's the point? I actually think they should ban them."

Tanner studied Remmy's face for a while and then sighed. He turned in his chair to stare out the window.

CHAPTER 2

As Thanner waited to see Commander Gaitee, he was coping with a sense of guilt. While he portrayed sadness for the benefit of his wife over his quick turnaround on assignments, he was secretly quite happy about it. He understood he was a natural-born romantic. The entirely safe and predictable life on Ambura was nearly maddening to him. That's why he chose the Space Service. Most avoided it because of the dangers – he chose it *because* of the dangers. On his assignments – particularly in his trouble-shooting division – very little was predictable ... and death was always a possibility. That element of chance and death added the emotion he desperately needed in his life. Remmy would never understand this – and would never forgive him if she knew his secret. Thus, the charade ... insincere but necessary.

An attractive woman exiting Commander Gaitee's office retrieved his mental focus from marital musings to present realities. She was a newbie. He was sure of it. Despite everyone on Ambura looking thirty-five, replacements were unmistakable. Youngsters, well under a hundred, had a demeanor and look in their eye that shouted youth. She looked at Thanner in a very brief, almost shy way, then speedily departed the outer office. A few minutes later, Gaitee opened his door and motioned Thanner inside.

Gaitee was about ten years older than Thanner, being one of the first wave of thirty-five year olds to get Fenzen. It was a funny thing, Thanner thought, as he looked at Gaitee ... we all look alike but you could always tell, somehow, who was older – and each assumed the role of junior or senior to the other. Gaitee sometimes overdid his slight age differential with highly affected gravitas ... but at other times, he was very easy going – just the

4

unpredictable personality type that drove Thanner crazy.
Gaitee, the senior in age and rank, spoke first.

"Nice to see you, Captain."

"Thank you, sir. Nice to see you."

"Nice job on Panetra ... saved us a lot of future trouble."

"Thank you, sir."

"Sorry about this quick turnaround, but you're the only
one I'd trust on this one. It's going to be very tricky – and
potentially very dangerous."

"It's all right, sir ... I'm always ready to help when
needed."

"That's what I like about you, Thanner – never any
complaints ... you just do your duty."

Thanner nodded in appreciation of the compliment.

"I was just going over the GXM 731 file. I'd forgotten
you were on a couple trouble-shooting missions there."

"They were both a while ago, sir."

"Yes they were."

"My first trip there was only my second mission."

"Oh really ... I didn't know that. I do remember it was a
real mess – a bloody mess."

"That it was. The Enrue command ship, with three
thousand voyagers on board, was vaporized."

"It's a good thing your crew was able to bring it down in
an uninhabited area."

"Yeah ... just killed a whole bunch of trees – and none
of the natives even knew it happened. They didn't even
discover the trees until many years later ... and concluded
it was an asteroid strike. That's what I call luck"

"That *was* a good bit of luck. They are *much* too
primitive to deal with the true reality of space. We weren't
so lucky on GRB 7165."

"That was a real shame. They're exposure to us
completely destroyed their culture and set them back many
thousands of years. Everything just fell apart. It's amazing
how fragile sentient psyches are. 7165 is the perfect case
study against those who argue for direct contact with the
primitives – as though we could just intervene and have
them jump thousands of years overnight. You can't
completely destroy a culture's set of beliefs then expect
them to survive ... just not realistic. The belief system is

5

the most essential element in any culture. Now if we could only convince the Olenreths of that."

"Frankly, it's irrelevant to them. They see something they want and to hell with anyone they hurt. It wasn't too bad when they would just toy with an isolated tribe. The tribe's culture would disintegrate but not the entire planet's. But when a planet reaches the stage, like 731 – where they have global communications – you can't keep an intervention local. We were just very, very lucky the last time. Can't count on that kind of luck every time. With what they have now on 731, they'd know all about another incident ... no matter where it happened. There are very few invisible areas there anymore – with all of the satellites they have. This time we'll have to proceed with great caution."

"Amen. So what are the details of the new mission, Commander?"

"It's about as bad as you can get. We just discovered the Olenreths have begun a trans-genetic program there."

"You've got to be kidding."

"I wish I was."

"That's an act of war, sir."

"Yes it is."

"Why would they do such a thing? Their entire sector could be attacked over this."

"I'm not sure ... I'd guess they thought nobody would catch them until it was too late."

"This is going to be a really difficult mission."

"That's why I picked you. We'll have to do interventions on this one ... no other way. I don't like these ... we could win the battle and lose the war, you know? You could weed out the trans-genetic subjects, but if you're not careful, you could disintegrate the entire culture in doing so. All I can say is – just be as careful as possible."

"Who's my First Mate, sir?"

"You're not going to be happy about it."

"Why?"

"First ... I want you to know it wasn't my decision. I opposed it ... but Sector Command wants to start integrating more Certificate Births into the missions –

particularly the trouble-shooting missions. Thinks we're discriminating against them."

"Don't tell me you're giving me a newbie!"

"I am. Sorry Thanner."

"On a mission like this?! They've got to be crazy!"

"I agree."

"Shit!! I just don't believe this. Well ... who's the newbie?"

"Lieutenant Vinta Zuly."

"A female?! Commander ... there's been an act of war. This is a combat mission, now. It's going to be very dangerous, with a good chance that someone might get killed. They've never sent a female on a combat mission before – ever. And not only a female – but a newbie female. She could get us killed."

"I said all that to Sector Command."

"How old is she?"

"Forty-two."

"She's practically a newborn ... seven years on Fenzen. Oh man. What experience does she have?"

"She's been on a couple of botanical missions."

"Oh ... that's great. Does she have any combat training?"

"Been to the Sector Combat School."

"Wow ... now I feel much better."

"Cut the sarcasm, Captain! You're in the service and you've got your orders, so shape up!"

"Yes sir. Sorry sir."

Thanner stared at the floor in silence, then finally spoke.

"I saw a wide-eyed, female newbie walking out of the office before I came in. Could that be Lieutenant Zuly? "

"Very perceptive. You're a real detective, Captain Plegrue."

Thanner ignored the sarcasm then spoke in a very military tone.

"When do we launch, Sir?"

"Four days. And if it makes you feel any better ... I arranged for you to get almost your entire regular crew back, for this mission. I had to pull some strings for that ... since it's rotation time."

"Is Iler with me?"

"Yes, he is. I made sure of that."

"Thank God. Maybe he can pick up the slack for the newbie."

"Captain ... look ... I know you're not happy with this ... I wouldn't be either. But please don't take it out on her ... OK? It's not her fault ... and if she complains about being treated poorly on this mission, it'll all come back on me."

"I'll deal with it, Commander, don't worry."

CHAPTER 3

On the 23rd of Anzu, Fenzen Era 162, Dangean Sector, Space Service Base DS 578, Planet Ambura, at 9:00 in the morning, the 25 member crew of the Enverton: Battleship Class, Space Bender, assembled in the Space Preparation Area for a briefing by Captain Thanner Plegrue, Ship Captain. Dressed in their day-class uniforms, they were drinking tea, snacking on an assortment of breakfast items, and quietly mingling while awaiting Capt. Plegrue's appearance. With the exception of two crew members, all had been with Capt. Plegrue on his last mission, which had returned to Ambura only ten days previous. There was one female – Lieutenant Vinta Zuly. The crew had not been advised of the inclusion of a female on this mission, and all were a bit perplexed as to her presence in the room. Some quietly advanced the proposition that she was probably some sort of specialist, brought in to give them some boring details about their planet destination. At 9:05, Capt. Plegrue strode through the open doorway. The first crew member to see him called the voyagers to attention.

"At ease. Please take your seats."

The crew quickly made their way to the chairs, arranged in a semi-circle around the podium, sitting in cliques of closest familiarity. Lieutenant Zuly and the other stranger sat together on the end seats to Plegrue's left. Capt. Plegrue placed his mission file on the podium and swept his glance along the entire crew from the right to left, smiling warmly. Except for the two new crew members, he had a very close emotional bond with the rest, having served together with them on ten missions over the past year. The collective grief over the tragic death of Weapons Officer Enton Biltra on the last mission drew them even closer together as something akin to a sacred brotherhood, which the death of a comrade can often do.

Thanner thought of this as he scanned their faces and poignantly realized just how difficult it would be for the new members to break into this special circle. The thought caused a pang of sympathy for them. He knew it would be even worse for Lieutenant Zuly.

"Good morning, crew."

A murmured mixed and pleasant response was replied.

"Well ... we just got home, and we're off again. We thought our last mission would be our last together for a good while, but here we are again. I can't tell you how pleased that makes me. As you noticed, I'm sure, we have two faces in the room."

He pointed to Lieutenant Zuly on the last chair to his left. All faces swung in her direction, awaiting the answer to their speculations.

"On my far left is Lieutenant Zuly. She will serve as the First Mate on this mission."

A murmur with clear tones of surprise and disapproval immediately emanated from the group.

"All right guys ... knock it off. Lieutenant Zuly is an officer in the Space Service and you will treat her with all due respect. I will tolerate no less. Is that understood?"

The men nodded in silence.

"I realize it is very unusual to include a female on a combat mission, but the Sector Command has confidence in Lieutenant Zuly, and I will respect their judgment and I will expect you to do the same."

Thanner paused to allow this admonition to sink in ... then continued.

"We also have Tenue Van as a new crew member. He was specially chosen for this mission. He is a member of the Advid Squadron and has distinguished himself in many combat missions."

The crew looked at one another with puzzlement, wondering why a member of the most elite Special Forces Unit in the sector would be accompanying them on this mission. It left them with a sense of foreboding.

"Since this is a classified mission, none of you have been briefed on the details. Here they are. Our destination is GXM 731. We have a very serious situation there. The Olenreths have committed a violation of the Avantrees

Accords. The violation is one that constitutes an act of war ... so we will proceed in our mission under the Universal Provisions of War. I will provide all of you with a copy of the Provisions and expect you to review them before our departure. To my knowledge, only Ensign Iler and I have been to 731. I've been there twice and Ensign Iler has been there once. Has anyone else been on 731?"

Faces looked back and forth then shook to convey a negative.

"OK. 731 is a no-contact planet. You all know what that means. No intervention is permitted by any sector with the natives. They have been designated as primitives and could suffer cultural disintegration through intervention. This is no bullshit, crew. I've witnessed the effects of intervention on primitives and it's a terrible thing. Anyway ... the Olenreths have not only intervened with the natives – they've undertaken trans-genetic activity with them. For those of you who don't know what this is ... it's when they begin interbreeding with the natives to produce a hybrid population that can live in the native atmosphere. They do this by capturing natives – male and female – and bringing them onboard a medical ship. They extract what they need from the natives, then implant the females with a combination of their own genetic material. After the female delivers the hybrid, they bring the infant and the male and female back onboard the ship. This time they extract genetic material from the infant ... do the mix of male, female, and Olenreth, and implant the female again. They keep going until they have a hybrid that can live in the native atmosphere but is essentially an Olenreth. It usually takes about four gestations to complete the genetic transfer. The final hybrid looks just like the natives, outwardly, but internally, it's Olenreth. When they have a sufficient hybrid population, they take over the planet and use it – and the natives – as they please. It's our mission to stop this program – by any means necessary, including elimination of the enemy – and to rid the population of all hybrids."

Thanner looked around the room to gauge how the crew was processing the information. There were looks of both concern and bewilderment. He knew he had to stop.

expect you to read it. We shove off in three days, so take care of your business and get ready. If anything comes up before then that requires a formal briefing, you'll hear from me. That will be all."

Lieutenant Zuly rose immediately to her feet and called the crew to attention.

The crew snapped to a formal, rigid, standing position and maintained their posture until Captain Plegrue left the room.

CHAPTER 4

Vinta Zuly ordered a salad and a glass of carbonated water, then handed her menu to the waitress with a warm smile. She then turned her smile toward Thanner Plegrue. He returned it. Thanner took a sip of his water then spoke.

"I'm really sorry I couldn't brief you before yesterday's crew briefing ... but I was under strict orders to keep details confidential because of the mission being on war status."

"I completely understand, Captain."

Look Vinta ... we're going to be commanding the ship together, so let's drop the titles ... OK?"

"OK."

"We're going to be spending a lot of time together on this mission, Vinta, and I think we should know something about one another before we shove off ... so that's why I asked you to go to lunch with me today. I've read your file ... but that doesn't really tell me much about you.'

Thanner waited for a response, but Vinta remained silent. To this, he thought of what a young kid she was. He went on.

"So ... you are all of forty-two, huh?"

Vinta blushed and looked down for a moment.

"Uh huh."

The phrase "Oh my God," went through Thanner's mind at this very youthful response to his question.

"Well then ... that makes me over a hundred years older that you. You know ... I haven't talked to a Certificate Birth for many years – and that was just a brief exchange. So, tell me ... what's it like to be a newbie?"

Vinta responded in a very quiet voice.

"It's very lonely, actually."

"Why?"

"Let's get on board and shove off. Our mission awaits." Lieutenant Zuly called the crew to attention then gave the appropriate commands to accomplish the prescribed manner of boarding a Space Service Ship of the Dangean Sector. The crew lined both sides the ship's ramp, twelve per side. Lieutenant Zuly stood at the top of the ramp, dead center, facing the boarding end. A few minutes later, Captain Plegrue emerged from the Space Preparation Area, executed a left flank movement and walked in military fashion the one hundred yards to the port area where the Enverton was docked. Upon reaching the ship's ramp, he executed a sharp right flank, took three steps forward and stopped just short of the ramp in a stiff position of attention. Ensign Iler, the first crew member on the Captain's right, shouted.

"Captain boarding!"

The crew instantly snapped their right fists to their chests and held them there. Captain Plegrue strode up the ramp and stopped just short of Lieutenant Zuly. She spoke in a loud voice.

"The ship is yours, Captain!"

She then took two steps to her right and Captain walked forward. He spoke as he passed her.

"Thank you, Lieutenant."

After the Captain had entered the Enverton, Lieutenant Zuly dropped her salute and stood with both arms stiffly at her sides.

"Crew of the Battleship Enverton ... you may now board."

The crew at the boarding-end of the ramp began marching up the ramp in single-file. They were joined by each consecutive crew member they passed. As each crew member approached Lieutenant Zuly, he brought his right hand to his chest in salute. Inside the immense ship, the voyagers went directly to their departure stations.

The officers of the ship assembled on the bridge on each side of Captain Plegrue. He spoke in a calm tone to Minveer Reg – the ship's chief pilot – who sat at a large, shiny metal table shaped in a half-circle and located about ten feet in front of the assembly. A very large, concave screen encircled the front of the table, displaying the view outside the Enverton.

"You may launch, Mr. Reg."

"Yes, Captain. Launching underway."

He touched a blue dot on the wide, flat panel sitting on the table in front of him ... engaging the anti-gravity drives. Reg then placed two fingers on a red bar display located on the far right side of the panel. He slowly moved his fingers a small distance toward the top of the panel and the concave screen showed the ship's forward movement. Having blocked the outward effects of gravity – while maintaining even gravity within the ship – the movement could not be felt by the crew ... at this speed or any other speed. The same was true of climbs, descents, or turns at any speed or angle. The ship could make a turn of ninety degrees, moving at near the speed of light, and its passengers would feel no sensation from the change of direction. It was very much like watching a video of a trip from one's own living room chair.

Thanner gave his next command.

"Advance to Fold Launch Position, Mr. Reg."

"Advancing to Fold Launch Position, Captain."

The pilot put the pointer finger of his left hand on a green dot – which indicated the Enverton's position – and his right pointer at a position on the panel about four inches above his left pointer.

"Advancing, sir."

Holding his right pointer in place, he quickly moved his left pointer to touch his right pointer. Traveling near the speed of light, the Enverton advanced 10,000 miles in an instant.

"Set position for GXM 731, Mr. Reg. Ten thousand miles spacing for arrival position. Place it on the dark side, Mr. Reg."

"Setting position for GXM 731. Ten thousand miles spacing for arrival position, dark side, Captain."

Reg inserted the appropriate galactic coordinates for GXM 731 in the ship navigator, attached to the right arm of his chair ... allowing for the 10,000 mile differential.

"Arrival position set, sir."

"Engage Space Folding Engines, Mr. Reg."

"Engaging Space Folding Engines, Captain."

Mr. Reg pressed the hieroglyph symbol on the screen for the Space Folding Engines. A noticeable hum immediately permeated the bridge and the crew could feel the vibrations under their feet.

"Space Folding Engines engaged, sir."

"Commence Fold, Mr. Reg."

The pilot, again, placed his left pointer finger on the Enverton dot then his right pointer on a large red dot about two feet from his left pointer.

"Commencing fold, sir."

Holding his right pointer in place, Reg moved his left pointer in a straight line to his right pointer.

"Fold complete sir."

In the center of the concave screen was a bright, shiny, blue sphere.

Thanner smiled.

"There she is ... GXM 731."

A jumble of excited comments immediately emanated from the officer corps.

Thanner looked at them.

"She's beautiful, isn't she?"

His First Mate spoke up.

"I've never seen a more beautiful planet, Captain. I can hardly wait to see her up close."

"You will, very shortly, Lieutenant Zuly."

"Set position for ocean base, Mr. Reg."

"Setting position for ocean base, Captain."

Reg inserted in the base's coordinates.

"Base position set, sir."

"Set a stop position for one thousand feet above the water surface, Mr. Reg. We'll go manual after that."

"Setting for one thousand feet altitude, Captain."

"Commence descent, Mr. Reg."

"Commencing descent, Captain."

Using his two pointer fingers on the screen, the distance from the arrival point and the prescribed altitude above the water was accomplished instantly. The curved screen was now black, except for some scattered moonlight, glittering on the waves.

"At altitude, sir."

"Engage night screen, Mr. Reg."

"Engaging night screen, Captain."

Touching another hieroglyph on the panel, the screen instantly displayed the ocean in vivid detail.

"Take manual control, Mr. Reg, and steer us to the base."

"Going manual, Captain. Steering to the base."

The assemblage watched the screen, intently, as the Enverton slowly descended toward the water. Ten seconds later, the ship was underwater and descending to the base – some ten miles into the deep. As they descended, they were witness to the plethora of marine life displayed on the screen, evoking many spontaneous remarks from the officers. After about ten minutes time, a huge, shining, transparent dome on the sea floor appeared in the distance. Thanner remarked.

"Well, crew ... there's home for a while."

As they were drawing closer, Thanner gave an order to the Communications Mate, sitting at his panel to the Captain's right.

"Dial up the base, Mr. Wenlen."

"Dialing up base, Captain."

"In contact, sir. Go ahead."

"This is Captain Plegrue, Battleship Enverton, Dangean Sector."

"GXM 731 Dangean Sector Base, Go ahead, sir."

"Request entry, Dangean Base."

"Entry granted, Captain Plegrue. Please proceed to port 43, sir."

"Will do. Thank you, Dangean Sector Base."

"You're welcome, Captain."

The pilot guided the Enverton downward and leveled off at about twenty feet from the ocean floor. He veered the ship to the right and traversed the outside of the immense dome, passing a number of ports along the way ... finally reaching port 43. The Enverton banked left and entered the high arched port entrance. They continued underwater for about a quarter of a mile, then ascended to the surface, beside a large boarding ramp. The pilot maneuvered the big battleship to a docked position.

"Enverton is docked, Captain."

"Shut down all engines, Mr. Reg. Excellent job."

"Thank you, sir."

"All engines down, sir."

Thanner looked at Lieutenant Zuly.

"Assemble the crew to disembark, First Mate."

"Yes, Captain."

CHAPTER 6

The crew of the Enverton was greeted by the Base Duty Officer. They boarded a suspended passenger vehicle. As it floated above its track, the crew's heads and eyes were constantly moving to take in as many of the sights as possible. The underwater base was a full-size replica of a typical Amburan city with houses, shopping areas, stadiums, avenues, parks, lakes, theaters – all landscaped with a decorative a variety of typical Amburan fauna and flora – from flowers, bushes, and grass to some trees, more than fifty feet in height. If the crew forgot, for the moment, that they were thousands of light years from Ambura, they could very well imagine they were still at home. It was nighttime inside the base as they rode the transport. Even though the outside water was perpetually black, the base lighting precisely replicated an Amburan day. The lighting created an Amburan sunrise with the typical yellow sky. The moving sun progressed through the daily stages until dusk then a star-filled, rotating, night sky appeared with the appropriate stages of the three Amburan moons. To avoid monotony, cloudy days and nights would sometimes appear ... occasionally accompanied by rain.

Lieutenant Zuly, sitting beside Captain Plegrue, leaned toward him to ask a question.

"Is this the same base where you stayed on your last trip here?"

"Yes ... it is."

"How long has it been?"

"Let's see ... about fifty years, I guess."

"Has it changed any?"

"Yeah ... quite a bit. There's a lot more landscaping than the last time ... and it's a lot prettier in general – homier. I remember some of the population complaining, last time, about how stark and military-looking it was.

They said it wasn't like this was a brief assignment ... most of the crews are here for quite a while – years at a time – and it needed to be more of a community. Looks as though somebody heard the complaints. This is really nice."

"It is ... it reminds me of Gonway. Have you ever been there?"

"Yes ... at the Weapons Training Facility."

"Me too ... that's where I was. Don't you think this looks like Gonway?"

Thanner looked around then shook his head in the affirmative.

"Yes ... now that you mention it – it does, somewhat."

"Are these all Amburans here?"

"Yeah ... they are. Too hard to accommodate all the races from across the Dangean Sector."

"Are there any other Dangean crews here?"

"Well, Vinta ... all that was in the briefing materials you were supposed to have read."

Vinta blushed and looked down. Thanner laughed.

"Don't worry ... I didn't read all that crap either. And another thing ... when it's just you and me talking, we agreed to drop the titles – remember?"

"Yes ... sorry Captain – I mean, Thanner."

"Back to your question ... we *are* the only Dangean crew here. The Amburan force is designated as the lead Dangean unit on 731. Of course, if things heat up with the Olenreths, all that could change very quickly, and we could have a lot of company down here. I'm not sure what kind of accommodations would have to be made for other Dangean units if they come, if they're not Amburan. They can't stay on this base ... it's not set up for their physiology – so I'm not sure what will be done. They may just have to stay on their ships. I've had to do that on other missions ... it's a real pain in the ass if it lasts for very long."

"I could imagine. I'd hate to be cooped up on the Enverton for very long. Not that it's not a nice ship ... I just suffer from claustrophobia if I'm locked up somewhere for long."

"I'm the same way. It even bothers me that – after the advent of space bending – they did away with windows on the inter-galactic ships. We can look any direction we want with our screens ... but it's just not like looking out of a window."

"Why was the Amburan force chosen to be the lead on 731?"

"The sector does its best to match the permanent unit with the native environment. They look at the atmosphere ... gravity ... and the native appearance. 731's atmosphere isn't a perfect match for us, but it's close. It allows us to wear converters instead of tanks. The gravity is heavier here than on Ambura. You'll notice it as soon as you're on the surface ... but you'll get used to it. Because of their gravity, the natives are considerably shorter than us. The tallest natives will only come up to about your chest. And their appearance ... it's remarkably close to ours – given that we're two thousand light years apart. Their faces are very similar to ours. Noses and ears are a little different. We both have hair on our heads – even though our hair strands are much thicker and our colors are different. Believe me ... you won't see dark green hair like yours – not naturally anyway – or a violet shade like mine."

"Can we pass for natives with some makeup and wigs?"

"No ... not really. I mean when you tower over all the natives and have almost no noses and tiny ears like we do ... it's hard to go unnoticed. All I can say is that we, at least, won't be completely repulsive to the natives – not like the Olenreths. They must have scared the hell out of the natives when they made contact."

"They *are* ugly as hell. I've seen better looking reptiles."

Thanner laughed.

"Funny thing is ... they think *we're* ugly as hell. I've heard them talk. They say that we look like some weird plant ... with our hair colors and orange-tinged faces. We call them 'Frog-Face' – they call us 'Weed-Heads.' And they think we stink."

"Really? I didn't know that. I figured they were ugly and were just all pissed-off about it."

"Oh, hell no ... they think they're beautiful."

"Oh my God ... you're kidding."

"You should hear them talking about their women."

"I don't even want to think about that."

Vinta visibly shuddered.

The vehicle stopped in front of a very large, pretty house that looked like a vacation villa that Amburan families rented for beach vacations. The crew disembarked, following Thanner, Vinta, and the Day Officer. Standing in front of this charming mansion, they looked at another with bewilderment on their faces. Thanner explained.

"Believe it or nor, crew ... this is our quarters. I read that they had done away with the typical barracks as part of their 'Amburan Village' initiative. Not bad, huh?"

With the commanding officers and the Day Officer in the lead, the smiling crew filed into their house. Inside, and standing in a spacious entryway, they looked around with even bigger smiles. The ceilings were very high, and large windows were everywhere. The floors were made of a colorful Amburan tile, and ahead of them was a wide staircase with an ornate banister done in an antique Amburan style. The Day Officer spoke.

"This is your home during your mission. We hope you enjoy it. All the rooms are on the second and third floors, and here is a list of the room assignments. Each room, you will notice, has a name – not a number. It's all a part of getting away from the barracks idea."

He handed the list to Thanner.

"If there's anything you need, just get in touch with our Base Services Office. You'll see the icon on the screens in your rooms."

He turned to Thanner.

"Any questions, Captain?"

"Only one ... when do we meet with Admiral Rite?"

The day Officer pressed a small screen on his wrist.

"At Eight Hundred-Thirty Hours, tomorrow sir."

"OK ... thank you. That's all, Ensign."

The Day Officer came to attention, executed a stiff salute, did a military about-face, and swiftly departed the house. The crew found their rooms, settled in, then came down to the kitchen and were very happy to find it well-stocked. After they ate, they split-up according to their inclinations. Some chose to stay in the house to chat, rest, read, play games, or watch television – choosing between either the base entertainment or captured native broadcasting. Others chose to go out into the artificially created Amburan night and enjoy the artificially created evening breezes.

CHAPTER 7

"How was your voyage, Captain?"

"Uneventful, Admiral."

"That's how it is these days with space folding. Sort of takes the adventure out of space travel, doesn't it?"

"It really does, sir. It's almost sterile, if you know what I mean. The voyage was always a significant part of the mission in the old days. Now you watch your pilot bring his two fingers together – and that's it. It's quick and safe ... but there's no heart in it."

"I totally agree ... but without space folding, we'd never be able to get to remote outposts like 731. With the old linear hibernation voyages, it would take a thousand years to get here. It's really opened up a lot more of the universe to us."

"That's true, sir."

"Well ... you're here for a mission, so let's get to it. Here's where we are. We only discovered the Olenreths' trans-genetic activities about a week ago. They don't know about our detection, yet. We want you to put them under surveillance and find out everything you can before we make a move. Once they know we're on to them, it'll be really hard to do any intelligence work."

"Is there anything, specifically, you want us to be looking for, Sir?"

"We have to find out who the trans-genetic subjects are ... then we've got to weed them out of the population."

"When you say, 'weed them out' ... are we talking about elimination?"

"Yes ... unfortunately. These are Olenreth mutants – and we can't let them get loose in the general population."

"To the natives ... these aren't mutants, sir. I'm sure they have no idea what was done to them on the Olenreths' medical ships – or that they were even on the ship. As far as the parents know, these children are completely normal."

"I know ... that's the shame in it. We're killing mutants – but to them it's their children."

Lieutenant Zuly put her hand to her mouth and Thanner could hear her take a quick gasp of air. He looked at her and held his gaze – long enough for her to get the message to keep her emotions under control. He realized, poignantly, at that moment, that Vinta Zuly was absolutely the wrong person for this mission. They were going to be killing beautiful little babies and he was sure it would be too much for her. He'd have to be ready to ask for a replacement as soon as this was apparent. Thanner had been on this sort of mission once before and knew how gut-wrenching it would be ... even for the most seasoned combat veterans. They were accustomed to killing adult soldiers – not babies.

Lieutenant Zuly asked a question.

"Excuse me, Admiral, if I may ... how will we know if all the mutants have been ... uh ... accounted for?"

She tried, but could not use, the word, "eliminated."

"We'll execute simultaneous boardings of all the Olenreth ships on 731 – and their base, as well – and seize all their records. That will tell us the location of every trans-genetic subject."

"Won't the boardings spark retaliation from the Olenreth Sector Command, Admiral?"

"That's a distinct possibility, Lieutenant. If that happens, we could have a Sector War on our hands. God help us."

With this statement, a silence came over the three. Thanner broke it.

"That could be a potential disaster for 731, sir."

"Indeed, it could. We were lucky with our last Sector War on 731. I read your file, Captain Plegrue. You were in on that."

"Yes sir ... it was one of my earliest missions. In that one, the Enrues backed off after we downed their command ship – and killed a few thousand voyagers with it. Let's hope it's that easy with this one ... if it happens."

"Any questions about the mission, Captain Plegrue?"

"No sir. The objectives are very clear."

Thanner looked at Vinta.

"Any questions, Lieutenant?"

Lieutenant Zuly shook her head in the negative and responded.

"No sir."

Admiral Rite looked at the two officers with an expression that indicated he was assessing the briefing and determining if there was anything else he needed to say. The sudden uplift of his head indicated that there was more.

"I want to stress that although we consider ourselves at war with the Olenreths, this must remain absolutely top secret. The longer they believe they are still undetected, the more time we have for surveillance. Make this absolutely clear to your crew, Captain. Not a word of this to anyone outside your group."

Thanner followed immediately.

"How do we explain why we're here, then, Admiral? When we show up it usually means there's trouble."

"Use the cover that you're here for a little R&R after your last mission ... after Enton's death and all. As a matter of fact ... I want you to go to the Pan-Sector Rec Base and socialize. Freely talk about how rough your last mission was and how much you all needed to just get away and relax for a while on this nice little planet. You can say you've been given permission to have some on-surface time in some remote locations. And make it a point to be friendly with the Olenreth contingent. They frequent the Rec Base quite a bit. Oh ... be sure to keep Tenue Van out of sight. He's a well-known Special Forces Commando and there's no good reason he should be here other than what he does best – which is not R&R."

"Are you clear on all of this, Captain?"

"Yes sir ... completely clear."

"All right then ... that will be all."

Instantly, Captain Plegrue and Lieutenant jumped to their feet in a stiff posture of attention. Simultaneously, they snapped a salute to their chests and held them there. The Admiral touched his fist to his chest with less stiffness and the officers snapped their fists to their sides in response. The Admiral commanded them.

"You're dismissed."

The two executed proper about-faces, in tandem, then walked stiffly out of the office with Captain Plegrue in the lead.

On their way back to their house, aboard a base transport, Vinta Zuly posed a question to Thanner.

"I was thinking, Thanner ... what we're about to do could end up destroying 731 in the event of a sector war, right?"

"That could happen."

"Then our intervention could doom the planet instead of helping it."

"Yes ... that's a possibility."

"Then ... why do this at all? Why not just let it go. At least the planet wouldn't be destroyed."

"Look Vinta ... if we just let it go – how do you think a belligerent race like the Olenreths would react?"

"What do you mean?"

"I mean ... if we let them go, on this ... why would they hesitate to do the same thing on other primitive planets?"

Vinta pondered this then responded.

"I see what you mean ... but it's just such a shame – doing what we're about to do. Killing babies."

"Vinta ... I want an honest answer. Are you going to be able to handle this mission?"

Vinta buried her face in her hands for some time. She finally emerged and answered.

"I think I can ... if I can just keep the reason for the mission in mind – that we have to stop the Olenreths from doing this here ... or anywhere else. The mission makes perfect sense – it's just blocking your natural emotions when you have a baby in your arms."

Vinta's eyes began to tear but she willed it to cease. Thanner continued.

"I had one other mission where I had to do this ... on another trans-genetic case. It was the hardest thing I ever had to do in my life. It really affected me – emotionally – for quite a long time. I had hoped I'd never have to do it again ... but here we are. You had better give this a lot of

thought before we begin operations. We had a couple of
crew members – males – on that trans-genetic mission that
just couldn't shake it. They ended up retiring from the
Space Service ... and have never been quite right since
then. So ... you had better be careful."
    "I have one question about this. Why is it necessary to
kill these children? I mean ... why can't we just take them
somewhere and let them live?"
    "Where would we take them Vinta? There not entirely
of the 731 race and they're not entirely Olenreth either ...
and we can't allow for the possibility that they might breed
with the general population.   So what are we supposed to
do with them?"
    Vinta shook her head.
    "I guess there's nowhere to take them. It just seems so
awful to take these innocent lives."
    "Vinta ... listen. I'm going to be blunt. I'm really not
sure I want you on this mission. I just don't think you're
going to be able to do this."
    "But if I can't handle my first mission with a trouble-
shooting crew ... my career in the Space Service is over."
    "Not really. You could get on another type of crew ...
botanical, sociological ... even a journalism crew. Lots of
other things you can do in the Space Service. You're with
the clean-up crew here. The only time they call us in is
when there's a mess ... and we have to clean it up. It's just
a dirty business – as you have just found out. Not
everyone is cut out for this kind of thing."
    "But I asked for this type of duty. I get bored so easily
and the scientific crews would drive me nuts. I was on a
couple of botanical missions and was so bored I cried."
    "Well, Vinta ... maybe you'll just have to find out for
yourself if you have what it takes for this kind of crew.
Just say the word and I'll assign you to a duty that keeps
you away from native contact and elimination activity. No
shame in that."
    "I appreciate that, Thanner, but I won't be coddled. I
want you to treat me just like you would any other First
Mate."
    "A First Mate's place is right by my side in everything
we do – no matter what we have to do."

"Then that's what I'll do."

"OK, Vinta ... but remember that sometimes you don't know what you're asking for when you ask for it. I've done my best to warn you."

"Yes you have, Thanner ... and I appreciate it. But I've made my decision."

CHAPTER 8

The crew of the Enverton saw the top of the inter-base shuttle emerge from the water and dock at the public station. They boarded the vessel, made of entirely transparent material, which then descended and moved backward toward the dock portal. Clearing the portal, it swung to its left and began moving forward. Having lights on all sides – top, bottom, left, and right – the crew had a panoramic view in every direction. They marveled at the abundance of life – plant and animal – that could live at such depths in the water ... so deep that had it not been for their lights, they would be in total darkness.

The shuttle passed by a number of massive sector bases, into which the crew could clearly see. Each was a microcosm of some planet within the base sector and each was dramatically different from the other bases. The shuttle slowed and turned right into the Pan-Sector Recreation Base. They ascended to the surface and docked. The crew disembarked and walked along a wide marble hallway, covered by a very high, multi-colored, arched ceiling. Entering the main base area, they could immediately feel the pull of gravity ... more than that of Ambura. They expected this. Most of the sector planets had more gravity than Ambura and the Rec Base catered to the majority of the sectors with bases on 731 – even though it was constructed by the Amburans, as the lead sector on 731. The crew also knew that they would tower over their fellow sector voyagers for the same gravity-related differences.

The base was panoply of landscapes from all sectors. The atmosphere was Amburan, so the Enverton crew wore no breathing apparatus. All other sector voyagers did ... some with simple converters – other with tanks. All wore a speech adaptor in an ear which translated any foreign

voice encountered into the listener's language. After
Captain Plegrue gave the crew a last, quiet admonishment
on protecting the secrecy of their mission, they broke into
smaller walking parties and departed to reconnoiter the
various areas of the base. Thanner and Vinta walked
together, heading toward a large, fresh water lake a few
hundred yards ahead of them. They nodded to passing
voyagers from foreign sectors. One group was Olenreth ...
to whom they not only nodded but bid them a good day
with pleasant smiles.

Suddenly Vinta stopped and put her hand to her heart.
Thanner stopped and stared at her, then looked in the
direction upon which she was fixed. On their right, sitting
on a sloped, grassy bank near the lake was an Amburan
couple. On the female's lap sat a very pretty, two-year-old
boy, giggling and playing with a fuzzy, toy danbler.
Thanner stared as well. It was more years than he could
remember since he had seen an Amburan toddler. It
tugged on his heart, as well. Vinta leaned in Thanner's
direction and almost whispered.

"Do you think they would let us hold him?"

Thanner shrugged.

"I don't know. Let's go see."

They both felt like running to the trio but managed to
look casual as they approached. Vinta spoke to the
mother.

"What a beautiful little boy."

The mother smiled.

"Thank you."

Vinta moved closer and sat on the grass a few feet from
the mother.

"What's his name?"

"Yother ... we call him Yotty."

Vinta leaned toward the little boy with a huge smile.

"Hi Yotty!"

Yotty beamed and extended his fuzzy danbler to Vinta.
She took it and overly admired it for the benefit of the
baby. He stuck out his hand for a return and as Vinta
gave it to him, she asked.

"Do you have an anbler, honey?"

The mother answered for her little boy, who could not yet talk, as Vinta was well aware.

"No ... but he gets excited every time he sees one. I suppose we'll have to get one, one of these days."

The mother looked at her husband then spoke continued.

"Sanla says no ... but I'm sure we will, eventually. He thinks they're too much trouble ... don't you honey?"

Her husband smiled.

"They are ... but you know women – they always find a way to get what they want ... especially for their children."

He looked at Thanner. Thanner smiled and nodded in a knowing way, then extended his hand and spoke while he shook Sanla's hand.

"I'm Thanner Plegrue. I'm with the crew of the Enverton."

"Hi Thanner. I'm Sanla Hilpen. I write for the Tanton Bylyn. I'm doing a story on 731. Are you staying on your ship or the base?"

"We're on the base."

"That's good. It's really very nice ... nicer than I anticipated."

"Yeah ... a lot more comfy than the ship."

"I could imagine. What class is the Enverton?"

"Battleship."

"Whoa! What's a battleship doing on 731?"

Thanner laughed.

"Don't worry ... no serious business. We got R&R here after our last mission. Now that was real battleship business."

"Glad you're getting some time off, Thanner. I wouldn't want to do what you do. It's good thing there are still people who will risk their lives to keep the rest of us safe."

Thanner smiled.

"Thank you."

He pointed to Vinta.

"This is My First Mate ... Vinta Zuly."

Sanla extended his hand to Vinta and she grasped it. He looked at his wife.

"This is my wife ... Kindo."

Vinta took Kindo's right hand in her two hands and held them warmly.

"Very nice to meet you, Kindo. Do you always get to come along on Sanla's trips?"

"No ... very rarely. But I had heard how pretty 731 is and really wanted to see it. I kept bugging Sanla until he asked his boss."

"Have you been on the surface?"

"Oh yes ... several times. It's gorgeous. We've been on number of deserted islands. The water is crystal clear ... and you can see all the bright colors on the bottom – blues, yellow, greens, reds. And then we got to land on a mountain. It was cold and had frozen water on it that was all white in tiny little particles. It was like walking on a pure, white beach. I've never seen anything like that. Yotty loved it. He picked up the white particles and threw them in the air ... then put it in his mouth. I went to stop him but Sanla said it was purified water and perfectly safe. Have you been here before?"

"Never. I can't wait go on the surface. But I must say – the Sector Base and the Rec Base are very, very nice."

"They are. I was kind of worried when Sanla told me we'd be in a base that's thousands of feet under the water ... but I was very pleasantly surprised. Would you like to hold Yotty, Vinta?"

Vinta put both of her hands on her heart.

"Oh my God, Kindo ... I'd love to hold him."

Kindo put her hands under Yotty's arms and extended him in Vinta's direction. Vinta took him and brought him to her chest. She laid his head against her, just under her chin then stroked the back of Yotty's head while embracing him with her other arm. Vinta's heart beat so fast she thought she might pass out with joy. Despite all her efforts, she couldn't stop the tears that began pouring from her eyes. She turned away so they couldn't see them. She had never held a child in her arms but her instincts were so strong it was as though she had given birth to the baby. Without thinking, she began to rhythmically sway and hum in his ear. Kindo watched Vinta and smiled to herself ... knowing that Vinta had never held a baby – like many women on Ambura.

With her back to the others, Vinta dabbed her eyes and sniffed. Her efforts to conceal were in vain, of course ... there being no way to hide this sort of thing, even with one's back turned. Finally realizing this, Vinta turned around and smiled at the other three with tears streaming down her face. Thinking she had overstayed Kindo's invitation to hold Yotty, Vinta carefully raised herself to a standing position, gave the cuddly baby a final, tender hug then extended him toward his smiling mother. Kondo – knowing how much it meant to Vinta, refused. She patted the ground to her left.

"Sit beside me. Hold him as long as you like."

Vinta lowered herself to the grass, very close to Kindo, and placed Yotty on her lap, facing her. She began gently bouncing him with her legs. She looked at Kindo.

"Do you mind if I ask how ..."

Kindo cut her off.

"It's OK ... everybody wants to know. We had a son. Anden was his name. He was killed three years ago."

Vinta put her right hand gently on Kindo's left shoulder.

"Oh ... I'm so sorry."

"Thank you. He was on a geological expedition on Wannendrew. He was killed in a landslide. It was heartbreaking. We thought we'd never get over it. He and Sanla were so close ... they did everything together. We had him for over a hundred years."

Kindo went silent and looked into the distance for a while. Finally she returned her gaze to Vinta.

"It's still so hard to talk about it. We were together for so long. They gave me my Replacement Certificate, but even the thought of having a new baby didn't make me happy. But the moment I saw Yotty's little face when they put him on my chest, my heart opened up again. I had completely forgotten what it was like to hold a new life in my arms. He's our whole life, now. I have nightmares about losing him – like we did Anden – but then I just pick him up and it all goes away."

Vinta put her arm around Kindo and pulled her close until the sides of their faces touched. A few moments later,

Vinta turned and kissed her forehead. She then whispered in her ear.

"God bless you."

Kindo snuggled her head against Vinta's and left it there for quite a while. The men smiled awkwardly at one another ... envying this moment that only two females could have – even two females who had just met one another.

CHAPTER 9

Thanner Plegrue set up round-the-clock surveillance of the Olenreth underwater base. He dispatched five single-crew ships to take up positions in a direct sight-line from the base, at a distance that would place them in complete darkness. When an Olenreth craft emerged from the base, the first designated surveillance ship would follow it at a safe distance, keeping a specific log of all activities and recording the coordinates of each movement. The crew member would also make video of any activity deemed pertinent. If all of the first squad of surveillance ships became engaged in pursuit, another group of five would be immediately dispatched to the surveillance point.

This mission was undertaken for one month. At that point, Captain Plegrue suspended it. All the data, accumulated by the surveillance teams, was turned over to the Enverton forensic group for analysis. After two days of analysis, they presented their findings to Captain Plegrue and his First Mate. It appeared that the daytime missions were engaged in typical tasks undertaken by most sector crews dispatched to a remote, primitive planet such as 731 – checking a variety of planetary gauges, gathering plant and animal specimens, photographing sites of interest, atmospheric testing, and general exploration and experimentation. Some of the nighttime missions were, however, not typical.

On a number of occasions, the Olenreth crews were observed descending to the planet surface in sparsely populated areas and, thereafter, seen entering native homes. The surveillance video showed the Olenreth crews departing the homes, carrying native bodies. They then took the bodies on board their crafts then to their underwater base. After several hours, they returned to the native homes and carried the bodies back into their homes.

The videos showed that the bodies were of adult males and females and, sometimes, infants.

With this intelligence, Captain Plegrue and Lieutenant Zuly set an appointment with Admiral Rite. After they briefed him on the situation, Admiral Rite continued to scan the intelligence they had transferred to his screen – stopping to study certain items for some period of time. The room was entirely silent. After a while, Rite pushed his chair back from his desk and leaned the side of his face into his open left hand. His left profile was toward the two officers and he stared at the distant wall of his large office. Finally, he swung his chair to his left and faced them.

"Here's what I want you to do. We need some concrete proof that the Olenreths are engaging in trans-genetics. It's obvious they are ... but we have no physical proof – only observations. We can't execute searches of their base and crafts without some physical evidence. We'd have hell to pay if we moved on them without it. So ... you'll have to make some surface landings and extract some infant subjects for testing. We need gene scans to prove the integration of Olenreth genes into their systems."

Thanner stared at Admiral Rite for a few moments then spoke.

"You only want the infants ... not the adults?"

"That's right. That's where the mixing is going on. The adults won't show us anything ... they're only using them for the eggs and sperm."

"How many subjects do you want us to extract, sir?"

"I'd get at least a dozen."

"What do you want us to do with the subjects after the testing?"

"Put them back where you found them ... and make sure you get the right infant with the right parents. We don't want any native panic and we don't want to tip our hand to the Olenreths at this point. I'll tell our surgeons to make sure any work they do is absolutely undetectable. Now listen ... you have to proceed with utmost caution. You've got to get into the home ... get the baby ... and get it out of there without detection. We know that these 731 infants cry very easily so you've got handle them properly. I'd suggest you have Lieutenant Zuly, here, handle them when you're in the home. Just like Amburan infants, these 731 babies respond more favorably to a female."

"Are there specific techniques we can use to keep the infant quiet?"

"Yes there are. I'll have some of our anthropologists talk to you about this. They have extracted quite a few of the items that 731 natives use with their offspring and they'll show you the techniques in using them. They also have quite a bit of video about 731 babies ... their behaviors ... the way the natives engage with them ... that sort of thing. You'll find that their parenting is very similar, in many ways, to Amburan parenting."

CHAPTER 10

Tyler McFarland slammed the door of his pickup truck and stared at the huge Wal-Mart sign on the building. He closed his eyes and shook his head back and forth many times. His mind was racing. He hated his job. He hated his manager. He would love to go back into the store ... walk up to Travis Henry and tell him to go fuck himself. He was trapped. He couldn't make a living on his farm anymore – with all the big corporate farms driving down the prices. He was forced to put up with idiots and demeaning work, just so he could make enough money to hold onto the farm. He could easily sell it to the neighboring corporate gargantuan but he just couldn't bring himself to do it. He was born there ... right in his mother's bedroom. He'd spent a halcyon youth on those three hundred acres, working side-by-side with his dad and granddad and his two brothers.

Tyler's older brothers, Tommy and Bill, were book smart. They studied hard, went to college and then some. Tommy was an architect in L.A. Bill was a pediatrician in Dallas. Tyler had no interest in college. To him, the farm was a paradise and he didn't understand why anyone raised on a farm would ever want to leave it. When someone could spend his life outdoors in the fresh air, working with his hands in the dirt, growing crops, and dealing with livestock who didn't argue with you ... why would anyone want to go anywhere else? He was happy where he was. He didn't have to go looking for happiness. His wife was just like him. She was raised on a farm only a few miles down the road and she loved it just as much as he did. Their dream was to raise a family and have their kids spend their childhoods just the way they had. They got married the summer after they graduated from high school.

Tyler and Annie moved into the big farmhouse with Tyler's parents and grandparents. They were ready to start a family. But it didn't start. Try as they may, Annie just didn't get pregnant. When he was twenty-five, Tyler's granddad died, and his grandma died a year later. When Tyler was twenty-seven, the corporate farms moved into the county and most of the neighbors read the writing on the wall – and sold-out. He and his dad held out. The four of them kept working the farm, trying to make a profit. They couldn't make it. His dad and mother were in their late sixties and decided to take what they had saved through the years and buy a home in a trailer park in Florida. They signed the deed over to Tyler and Annie and left.

Annie got a job at a bakery. Between the two of them them, they made just enough to pay the real estate taxes and for enough seed to make a little money on twenty acres of corn. Their few remaining chickens kept them in fresh eggs and one cow gave them their milk. Despite their troubles, they were still in love. When they were both twenty-nine, a miracle happened. One Friday evening, Tyler came home from work to find Annie crying in the living room. He ran to her and held her, asking her over and over what had happened. She pulled away from him and started laughing harder than he had ever seen. Tyler stared at her ... thinking she had truly lost her mind. Suddenly she held up what appeared to be a small strip of paper between her thumb and forefinger of her right hand and started dancing around the room. Totally baffled, Tyler folded his arms across his chest and just watched her. Finally she danced over to him and handed him the small strip and danced away. He held it between his fingers and studied it. He looked at her, just as perplexed at he had been, shaking his head with a look of inquiry on his face. Annie stopped her dancing and put her hands behind her back. She began swaying back and forth and broke into song.

"We're gonna have a baby ... we're gonna have a baby ..."

Tyler was speechless. The moment felt unreal. The resolved story of their lives for many years was that she was just one of those women who couldn't have a baby. Her singing seemed almost a mockery of their reality. His mouth hung open as he stared at her. She came to him and wrapped her arms around his waist. She looked into his eyes. Her mouth curved into a serene smile and she spoke in a soft voice, nearly a whisper.

"Honey ... we're going to have a baby. You and I ... a little baby."

"But ... how ... you're ..."

"I know sweetheart. I can't have a baby ... but I'm having one."

"How is that possible, Annie?"

"I don't know and I don't care. Call it a miracle. Or call it an answered prayer. Either way ... we're having a baby."

"How do you know ... for sure?"

She pointed to the strip he held in his fingers.

"That's the fifth strip I used."

Tyler looked at the strip.

"What is this thing?"

Annie laughed and playfully pounded Tyler on the chest.

"You *are* a farm boy, Tyler McFarland. Are you serious that you don't know what that is?"

"I'm serious."

"You've never seen one of those on the commercials?"

"Not that I ever recall."

She took the strip from his hand.

"Well, honey ... you see ... when a girl thinks she's pregnant, she pees in a cup and sticks one of these strips in the pee. If the strip turns red ... she's pregnant. And I've turned five strips red. And I called Dr. England and asked him. He said if it worked that many times ... there's no doubt about it."

In that instant, their world totally changed. Their future had been the tale of the solitary couple, struggling together on a crumbling farm and aging in dignity until the first death ... soon followed by the second. With one event, their future was completely and joyfully rewritten. It was a metamorphosis ... a lowly caterpillar transformed into a wondrous vision on gossamer wings. A baby! Crisscrossing thoughts raced through Tyler's mind in a jumble of glory. A son to work with him ... a daughter to grow beautiful before his eyes ... the Christmases ... birthday parties ... proud visits to Florida. His chest felt too small to contain his swelling heart.

Tyler wrapped his sturdy, farm-boy arms around Annie and squeezed her – probably too tightly. Clumsy as he was, they bounced around the room in this tight embrace until they tripped on the throw rug and fell in a happy heap to the floor. Tyler instantly stiffened and looked with panic into Annie's eyes. She immediately understood the future father's terror and reassured him.

"I'm fine, honey ... don't worry. He's tucked away in a very safe place."

Tyler flashed a wry smile and Annie looked puzzled ... then got it.

"Did I say, 'he'?"

"You sure did.'

Annie gave her head a contemplative tilt.

"Now why would I have said that?"

"Don't know, honey ... maybe mother's intuition. "

"Guess we'll see ... won't we?"

Tyler put a big, calloused hand on each side of her face and pressed his lips to hers in a big, hearty-mouthed kiss – unlike any kiss he'd given her for many years. It was a kiss of love, friendship, partnership, and of companionship through many troubled waters. If there were love greater than that which enveloped these farm kids at that moment, no one could ever convince them of it. Annie leaped onto the couch, curled her legs under, as only females can do, and patted the couch beside her while prompting Tyler.

"Let's talk."

Tyler plopped himself on the same cushion with Annie and they launched into the silly, dramatically premature, cacophonous prattle that takes place between all couples expecting their first baby. Jumping among topics and never finishing any of them, they worked through the retinue of the baby world ... the nursery, names, boy or girl, whether to find out during the ultra-sound, who it will look like, preschool or not, when to tell their parents, what it would become in life, preferred and forbidden sports, cheerleader or athlete, scholar or farmer, which pediatrician ...

After nearly two hours of nonstop verbiage, the steam ran out of the kettle and they finally lapsed into a quiet reverie of silent contemplation – each envisioning a unique dream.

The next morning, at breakfast, their conversation lurched toward the practical. Tyler started it.

"Do you think you should quit your job, honey?"

Annie laughed.

"Sweetheart ... I'm not an invalid. Not yet, anyway. I'll be fine for quite a while. When it gets too hard to stand on my feet, we'll talk about it."

"Are you sure? Maybe being around all that flour and hot ovens could be dangerous for the baby."

Annie patted Tyler's huge forearm.

"Don't get crazy on me, baby doll."

Tyler laughed at himself. Then Annie grew serious.

"We do need to talk about after the baby's born. Things are tight now ... a baby will make things even more difficult."

"Well ... one thing for sure – you're staying home with the baby. No daycare for us."

"I'd love that more than anything, Ty ... but can we afford it?"

"I don't care what I have to do ... work two jobs ... it doesn't matter. I'll do whatever I have to do so you can be home with the baby."

Annie nodded and gave a quiet smile to Tyler.

"OK honey."

Tyler studied Annie's face as he considered his next thought.

"Maybe we should consider selling off some of our acreage."

Annie shook her head in the negative.

"Only as a last resort, honey. We swore to one another that we'd never break up the farm. Even though I know they had to do it, I'll never forgive my parents for doing that to our farm. All those beautiful acres turned into a housing development for the corporate workers. They put a lot of money in the bank, but look at how they live now, surrounded by cookie-cutter homes. The only upside of it was that – if we really had to – we could borrow some money from them."

"No way, Annie! I told you that! I'll never borrow a dime from anybody – especially your parents. What kind of a husband would that make me?"

"I know Ty ... I know. I'm sorry. I just keep that in mind when I get really scared about our bills."

"You just don't worry. We'll find a way. We always have."

CHAPTER 11

Each day of Annie's pregnancy was pure joy for the couple – even the early days of nausea and vomiting then the times of painful breasts, aching back, and chronic heartburn. They had waited and prayed for so long to have a baby, no sickness or pain could overcome their unbounded happiness. The only troubling times they experienced were unrelated to the baby. At about the sixth month they both began to have nightmares. Neither had ever had a nightmare, but these were so real and terrifying they didn't dissolve upon awakening. Both avoided any mention of these until they could no longer be borne in solitude. It became more frightening when each discovered that not only were they both plagued with nightmares, but that they were experiencing the exact same nightmare – horrible visions of the some reptilian creatures taking them from their beds to some kind of examination room. Night after night these creatures visited their sleep, to the point that neither wanted to go to sleep. Annie finally convinced Tyler that they needed to see someone about it. Being of hearty farm stock, neither of them had ever been to the doctor's office for anything but a few injuries, excepting the pregnancy – Tyler for a broken arm then a badly twisted knee ... Annie for a concussion resulting from a horse kick. Annie took the tack of stressing the possible effect her lack of sleep might be having on the baby and that she needed Tyler there to help describe the problem.

Dr. English gave them both a complete physical exam with blood work. Tyler thought this was entirely stupid but went along with it to pacify Annie. English proclaimed them both to be physically fit. He then suggested they see a psychologist. Tyler drew the line on this and absolutely refused, so Annie, for the baby's sake, went alone. Tyler drove her the seventy-five miles to downtown Omaha and waited in a nearby park while Annie went to the medical arts complex to see Dr. Anthony. She returned about ninety minutes later and sat on the bench with Tyler. As soon as she was seated, Tyler asked her what the doctor had to say. Annie took a while before speaking ... deciding just how to word her response.

"He was really puzzled that both of us were having the exact same nightmare ... said it was highly unusual. Not only that we're both having the same nightmare but that neither of us has ever had nightmares, before. He said he'd never, personally, seen a case like this. Then ..."

Annie stopped abruptly. This drew Tyler's focused attention.

"What?"

"You don't even want to hear this."

"Well now that you brought it up, you better say something."

"You're gonna get mad."

"I'm gonna get mad if you don't tell me what it is."

Annie moved her vision around her, from the sidewalk to the trees above, to her fingernails then to Tyler's eyes – and fixed them there.

"OK ... here it is. He said the only thing similar to this he's ever read about are cases of alien abductions."

"What the hell is that?"

"You know ... the stuff I watch on Discovery and the History Channel."

"Are you talking about that UFO bullshit you like to watch all the time?"

"Yes."

"Jesus Christ, Annie ... do you mean to tell me that I drove you seventy-five miles and spent a hundred-fifty dollars – we don't have – to have some guy tell you we were abducted by creatures from Mars?"

To diffuse the situation, Annie smiled and tried some humor.

"There aren't any creatures on Mars, Tyler."

It didn't work.

"That's very funny, Annie. I'm serious here ... what kind of help is that ... bringing up that kind of crap?"

"He was only telling me his experience – that the only people having these kind of nightmares – the same one by two people – about strange creatures taking you away and examining you – are the ones who say they have been abducted."

"Even if that's the only thing that he knows is close to our situation, what good is it to bring it up? It's all just bullshit."

Annie looked at him with a slightly lowered face and a sheepish look.

"He wants me to see a psychologist that specializes in this sort of thing."

"What sort of thing?"

"You know ... alien abductions."

"Oh yeah ... I'm going to spend another hundred-fifty on a guy who actually thinks people get abducted by aliens. He oughta be paying some other psychologist to help him find out how *he* went nuts. He'll probably try to get you to be on one of those UFO shows you watch ... you know when they hypnotize you and get you to tell some crazy story."

"Well ... regardless of what you say, Tyler, I'm going to do it. I need some help ... I can't keep going on like this. I've never been happier in my life with our having a baby ... and this is taking some of that joy away from me. It's not fair. I can't ..."

Annie burst into tears. Tyler threw his arms around her and held her tightly.

After she calmed down, Annie wiped her eyes, blew her nose, folded her hands in her lap, then calmly looked Tyler in the eyes.

"Tyler ... listen ... I admit this may sound crazy to you ... but how do *you* explain what's going on? How do you explain that we are all of a sudden having nightmares – and neither of us have ever had nightmares before – and we're having the exact same nightmare? What's your explanation for something as strange as this is?"

Tyler crossed his arms across his chest and looked down in contemplation. After a while, he blew air out of his mouth and inflated his cheeks. Without looking at Annie, he responded.

"I don't have one, Annie. It's a totally crazy thing. There's just no way to explain it."

He paused and turned to look Annie in the face. He spoke without emotion.

"But just because I can't explain it doesn't mean that we've been abducted by aliens from outer space ... does it?"

Annie shook her head in the negative and responded in the same, emotionless tone.

"No ... it doesn't prove we were abducted ... but at least it's the explanation that some very well-educated people have come up with for people who have had the exact same experience as us. I don't know of any other explanations that have been offered to explain our very weird situation ... do you?"

Tyler raised his hands, palms upward, and spoke in a tone of resignation.

"No ... I don't Annie."

CHAPTER 12

Two weeks later, Tyler and Annie McFarland got up at 5:00 a.m. and were on the road at 6:00, to begin the three-hour drive to Kansas City to see Dr. Lewis Dryden, Clinical Psychologist, Specialist in Alien Abductions. During the interim between the last visit to the psychologist and this one, Annie had prevailed upon Tyler to join her in seeing Dr. Dryden. She had also extracted a clarion avowal that he would – in no way – act in an antagonistic, sarcastic, or flippant manner toward the doctor. At 9:03 they pulled into a white-lined parking place on the third floor of the garage attached to the hospital in which Dr. Dryden's office was located. Having a 10:00 appointment, they pressed the elevator button for the hospital lobby in the possibility of finding a snack bar. The possibility became a reality, and they sat at the counter and ordered coffee. At 9:45, they took the hospital elevator to the fifth floor, and followed the room number signs to Suite 522. Before they reached the door, Annie stopped and took Tyler by both of his hands.

"Honey ... remember what you promised. I really need you to take this seriously. Please do this for me. OK?"

"Don't worry. I'll be a good boy."

Annie slid her arms around Tyler and squeezed him hard with her farm-girl muscles. They checked in with the young woman at the window and took a seat. At ten o'clock, promptly, a door to the right of the reception window opened and a tall, casually dressed, athletic man in his forties stood in the doorway, holding it open. He smiled warmly and spoke to Annie and Tyler.

"C'mon in."

Tyler was surprised by the man's appearance. He expected an older, grayer man with a beard and glasses in a lab coat. They followed him along the hallway with a right then a left turn. He stopped at an open door and extended his left hand for them to enter the room. There were three comfortable, cloth-upholstered chairs arranged in a circle.

Dr. Dryden extended his right arm toward the chairs. "Take your pick."

As usual, Annie followed Tyler. He picked a chair and sat down. Annie sat to his left. Dr. Dryden took the remaining chair. Tyler figured this was some kind of test ... that their manner and choice of chairs probably meant something in the psychological realm.

Dr. Dryden spent the first forty-five minutes getting to know the McFarlands – their childhoods, families, their marriage, jobs, and finally, the pregnancy and baby plans. Tyler was becoming inwardly exasperated. They were spending two hundred dollars for a ninety minute session and here they were, chatting about minutiae, like neighbors over the fence.

Finally, Dr. Dryden got around to the nightmares, asking first about the time frame. When did they begin? Six weeks ago. Who had the first nightmare? Annie. When did Tyler's begin? Two days later. How often do they occur? Almost every night. Was anything significant going on in their lives at the time the nightmares began, other than the pregnancy? No. Do the nightmares vary from night to night? No.

Dr. Dryden turned to Tyler and asked him to describe everything he could remember about his nightmares.

Tyler looked up at the ceiling to compose his thoughts.

"Well ... it always starts with Annie waking me up at night by pushing me, really hard, on my right shoulder. I'm kind of aggravated about it. I look at her face and she looks terrified about something. Then I look up and see six big things standing all around the bed."

"Can you describe them?"

"Not real well because there isn't much light in the room – the only light is from the night light on in the bathroom."

"Where's the bathroom from your bed?"

"It's out our bedroom door and down the hall a few feet. So ... what little light there is ... is coming from behind them."

"OK ... go ahead."

"They have some kind of suits on ... with round helmets. I can't see their faces. I try to get up and grab the one beside me but he throws me down on the bed like I was a rag doll. Like a gorilla grabbing me. Strong as hell. Then they're all over both of us ... grabbing us and holding us down. The next thing I know, I'm in a really bright room and I'm strapped down on a hard table. I don't have any clothes on but I'm not cold ... it's really hot in the room. I'm laying there – alone in the room – for a long time. Then three of these things come into the room. They're wearing what looks like what these Arabs wear ... a long, thin thing that goes to the floor. A yellow color. They're built like gorillas ... really big shoulders and not very tall. Their faces are awful. Their skin is a brownish-green and smooth and shiny – like a frog. That's what their faces reminded me of – a frog. Really wide mouths with no lips and two holes – for noses, I guess. Big eyes. Looked almost black. Just slits around them ... no eyebrows or eyelashes. No ears. No hair anywhere. Their arms were thick and muscular, covered with the same frog skin. But their fingers were long and thin. Didn't seem to go with their bodies. Only had four fingers. One thumb and three fingers. Then the one that's standing at the end of the table, near my feet, starts handling my balls and my dick ... looking really close at them. His fingers are really cold. I start screaming at him."

"What do you say?"

"I say ... 'Get the fuck away from me, you cocksucker'"

Dr. Dryden smiled.

"Does he say anything to you?"

"No. He just points at something behind me. The gorilla frog, on my left, leaves and comes back with some shiny metal thing that looks like big ballpoint pen. He puts the pointed end of the thing against the side of my head. The next thing I know it's morning and I'm laying in bed beside Annie. That's it. Same thing every night. I'm telling you what the dream was about but not how I feel

when I'm dreaming. I'm terrified the whole time. So
scared I can't even describe it. That's about it."
"How about you, Annie?"
Annie was silent for an uncomfortable length of time.
Just as Dr. Dryden appeared to be ready to prompt her
again, she spoke.
"I have to say something, Dr. Dryden. I talked Tyler
into coming with me for this visit – and made him promise
not to be a smart aleck about anything that goes on ... but
I need to say that I'm feeling really stupid right now."
"Why?"
"While I was sitting hear ... listening to Tyler ... he
sounded just like all these people I've watched on the UFO
programs on TV ... talking about their abductions. I
almost started laughing. You know ... the creepy people
standing around your bed ... being strapped to a table with
these aliens examining you and doing repulsive things to
your body. I feel like I'm on television. I'm beginning to
think that people like me – who watch these UFO programs
all the time – see these stories so many times that we start
dreaming about what we've seen on TV."
"Is that what you think is causing you and Tyler to
have these nightmares?"
"For me ... yes, maybe. But not for Tyler. He won't
watch those programs. He'll go do something else if a UFO
program comes on. I don't think there's any way he's
having these nightmares because of television. But it's
almost the exact script from a UFO program when he's
talking about it. I don't know what to think. It just feels
dumb hearing Tyler's story."
"Well ... one thing I always try to determine with a
patient is the possibility of exactly what you're talking
about – that you could have been influenced by things
you've seen and heard. Let me ask you this ... how long
have you been watching these programs?"
"Oh ... for years – since I was a teenager. I've always
been into UFO's and outer space stuff ... like the shows
about the universe and that old program, NOVA, I think it
was called. I saw all of the Star Trek movies ... and Star
Wars, too. I'm a big fan of Starship Galactica."

"And have you ever had any dreams about outer space or space aliens before this recent bout with nightmares?"

"No ... never."

"So is there any reason you can think of that these nightmares would start now?"

"The only new thing going on, is me being pregnant ... that's about it. Let me ask you something, doctor. You're an expert on alien abductions and I guess you've talked to lots and lots of people who think they've been abducted by space aliens ... so do you think the story Tyler just told you sounds like what you hear from a lot of the other people you see?"

"Yes ... it does. People who have had these dreams, often have almost the exact same experience that Tyler just described. Not all of them have dreams. Some of them have waking flashbacks about these things and with hypnotic regression, they provide details like Tyler did about his dreams."

"Have you ever been on one of the abduction programs on TV?"

"Yes ... I've been on several."

"I knew it! I knew I'd seen you somewhere before. They showed you doing some of those hypnosis things."

"Yes ... that's right, they did."

"I have to ask you this. Are you doing this sort of thing – like seeing Tyler and me – just so you can go on TV and talk about it?"

Dr. Dryden laughed.

"Annie ... I've been doing this sort of thing long before anyone started putting on any programs about it. I only agreed to be on television a few times to bring this sort of thing out of the shadows and let people know they aren't the only ones experiencing these kinds of dreams and flashbacks. I happen to think that the reason these stories are so similar is because this is a real phenomenon and the method by which aliens abduct people is pretty much the same."

"Why are you so convinced it's a real thing?"

"Psychologists and psychiatrists all over the world have patients coming to them and telling them these exact, same stories ... many from countries where very few people

have television or where it's only state-run TV that
certainly doesn't have programs about UFO's. There's just
too much consistent evidence of this phenomenon to
conclude anything else but that it's a real thing."

"So if aliens from outer space are regularly abducting
people from Earth ... why are they doing it?"

"That's the fascinating question, Annie. My personal
opinion is that it's curiosity. To advanced civilizations,
we're a lower-life species ... just like explorers on Earth
going into the Amazon rain forest and collecting new and
strange animals. We bring them home and examine them
and do tests on them – all because of our innate curiosity."

"So are you saying that Tyler and I may really have
been taken out of our bed by aliens and examined
somewhere?"

"It's a possibility, Annie. In your case, if it were only
you having these nightmares, I'd suspect it could be the
affect of your TV watching. But with Tyler having these
dreams – and you having the same dreams – I'd rule out
the TV effect and look for other explanations. As for other
explanations ... I'd say that I'd put my odds on an actual
abduction."

Tyler jumped into the conversation.

"Jesus Christ, Doc! I don't know about Annie – but
you're scarin' the shit outta me! I came here to help Annie
feel better – and now you've got us worried that we were
actually abducted by space aliens! What are you trying to
do to us? Make us crazy!?"

"Not at all, Tyler. I'm trying to help you deal with your
nightmares. I think it's better to deal with reality than give
you some mumbo-jumbo that this was some kind of
Freudian manifestation, stemming from your childhoods.
From what I can see of your personalities and backgrounds
... there's no underlying psychological reason you should
be having these nightmares – particularly having a parallel
experience with identical nightmares. That would make no
sense to me. I think you may have to begin to cope with
the real probability that you were, in fact, abducted. Now,
that's a hard and scary thing to face ... but at least it's
something tangible to deal with. Neither one of you is
psychologically unbalanced, and you don't need any help

in that capacity. The only help I think I can extend to you is assisting you to cope with the probability that you were abducted. If you simply can't accept that possibility ... then there isn't much I can do for you."

Tyler and Annie looked at one another and communicated with their eyes. Annie spoke for them.

"I think Tyler and I need to talk about this before we make a decision on what to do. Now, we live quite a distance from here, and making another trip would be very difficult for us ... especially with me being seven months pregnant. So is there any possibility we could get a room – here in town – and let you know tomorrow ... and if we decide to go ahead and talk with you about this ... do you have time to see us tomorrow?"

"I'll tell you what. If you two decide you want to see me tomorrow ... I'll stay after my usual hours and see you then – which would be after five o'clock. How's that?"

Annie looked at Tyler and got his silent assent.

"They would be just fine, Dr. Dryden. That's very nice of you."

"OK ... then that's what we'll do. Do me a favor ... and let me know by noon what you want to do so I can plan my day ... OK?"

"Oh sure ... we will."

CHAPTER 13

Remembering having passed a Comfort Inn on the interstate just before Kansas City, the McFarlands retraced their journey and checked in. Neither having eaten since breakfast, they immediately went to the Bob Evans beside the hotel and devoured sizeable meals in short time with no chit-chat – typical of hungry farmers. Their immediate needs satiated, they got coffee refills and engaged in conversation. Annie began.

"What did you think of Dr. Dryden, honey?"

"He wasn't what I expected. When I think of a psychologist, I picture some goofy professor guy with a lab coat on ... smoking a pipe."

Annie laughed out loud and playfully slapped his forearm.

"Are you kidding? You've seen too many movies, you silly boy."

Tyler smiled at Annie's affectionate tone.

"Yeah ... I guess. But I actually liked him. I was all prepared not to ... but I did. He was much younger and more athletic-looking than what I thought a psychologist would be."

"I liked him, too."

"I was really surprised when you went after him the way you did. That's not like you."

"I surprised myself. I started feeling bad about it as I was talking."

"I'm glad you said what you did, cause I was thinking the same thing. Of course ... if I had said what you said, you'd have been all pissed off at me."

Annie smiled.

"Yes ... I would have. You were a very good boy, Tyler McFarland. You kept your word."

"Thanks, Mom."

Annie chuckled.

"Well ... what do you think?"

"About going back?"

"Yep."

"Geez ... I don't know, Annie. What he said really spooked me. Don't you think that's scary as hell ... that he thinks we were actually abducted?"

"I sure do. It makes my skin crawl. But it's like ... unless we accept that we were abducted, he doesn't want to talk to us anymore. On one hand ... I understand what he's saying. There's no good reason we should – all of a sudden – both be having the same nightmare ... and that something must have happened to both of us to cause this. But to go from that, to accepting the fact that we were abducted is a big and scary jump."

"I'll tell ya, Annie ... if I were to accept that we were actually abducted by aliens from some other planet ... I don't know what I'd do. I don't think I'd want to live in our house anymore. Knowing that they could come and get us again is just too creepy. And if we had a baby in the house ... how safe would *you* feel?"

"I know, Tyler. That's how I feel. Just thinking that those creatures were real – and that they were in our house and were touching us..."

Annie visibly shuddered then continued.

"I feel so invaded just thinking about it. Almost like I was raped. And with a baby coming ... oh my God, Tyler. I'd never get any sleep, worrying."

Both became silent for quiet a while. Tyler broke it. He stared Annie in the eyes.

"Do *you* think we really could have been abducted?"

Annie held his stare as she thought. She put both her hands to her mouth and leaned back against the cushion of the booth seat while still holding her fix on Tyler. Then she began shaking her head back and forth with her hands still on her mouth. She slid her hands down just low enough to speak.

"I don't want to think that, Tyler ... I just don't want to."

"I don't want to either, Annie ... but that's not what I asked you."

Fear spread across Annie's face, she spoke in a voice just above a whisper.

"Do *you* think we were, Tyler?"

"I think – logically – we could have been. I can't think of any other explanation. Can you? I mean ... something had to have happened to us. I actually can't believe I'm saying this ... but that's what I think."

Annie covered her entire face with her hands and kept them there. She began shaking her head in small, quick motions and Tyler could make out her slight moaning.

He leaned across the table.

"Are you OK, honey?"

She quickly dropped her hands and her face was a combination of fear and anger. When she spoke, the anger was foremost.

"Of course I'm not OK!! What do you think!! Our house was probably invaded by those ugly monsters and they had their hands all over us!! And you ask me if I'm OK!! Are you fucking kidding me!!"

Tyler drew back in shock. He had never in his life heard Annie use any profanity, and she was shouting in the restaurant. He had never seen her like this. He looked around at the other tables to find everyone looking at them. He was embarrassed and bewildered as to what to do. He wanted to get the hell out of their as soon as possible. He leaned toward Annie.

"Honey ... shhh ... please. Everyone's looking at us."

She jumped to her feet and shouted.

"I don't care!! Let them look!!!"

She put her hands over her mouth and nose and ran to the ladies room. Tyler put his elbow on the table and his hand to his forehead as he surreptitiously looked around at the people near him. Finding them all gaping at him, he simply looked down at his paper placemat and kept his eyes there. About ten minutes later, Annie returned to the table. She grabbed her purse from the table and spoke in a matter-of-fact tone.

"Let's go, Tyler."

Without looking at anyone in the restaurant, they made their way to the cashier.

CHAPTER 14

Annie issued not a word as she walked ahead of Tyler to the hotel, through the door and lobby, on the elevator ride, into the room, then into the bathroom. An hour later, the door was still closed. Tyler had heard the sound of the bathtub being filled but nothing thereafter. After about a half-hour more of waiting, he considered turning on the TV to watch Fox News ... but decided against it lest Annie might emerge and deride his "casually amusing himself" with television while she was so distraught. As an alternative, he went down to the lobby and got a complimentary copy of USA Today. He figured reading a newspaper would be considered less of an offense.

As usual, Tyler McFarland could not figure out how he had become the target of Annie's anger. All he did was answer her question about alien abduction. He was flummoxed as to how this made him the bad guy. He allowed this line of questioning to quickly subside, however – as he always did with Annie – under the general banner of female mystique. Over the years, he had often seen his mother erupt unexplainably at his dad. He would stare questioningly at his dad ... to which he would receive a shoulder shrug and an expression of resignation. After being married for a good while, he understood his dad's communication completely. It said, "I don't get it ... I never will ... so let it go." He knew, at some point – as long as he acted contrite for some sin he didn't commit – Annie would recover, return to normal, and the subject would never be discussed nor explained.

By about ten o'clock that evening, after Annie had emerged from her bathroom fortress, put on her pajamas, brushed her hair and filed her nails, she was back to normal. Annie always packed an overnight bag for herself whenever they went out of town – just in case. This trip turned out to be a just-in-case trip. He wished he had packed an overnight bag. He could, at least, use her toothpaste and swish out his mouth. He later discovered the notice on the sink about the front desk having bathroom essentials and went down to the lobby and got a complimentary razor, deodorant, and toothbrush.

Annie asked Tyler, very pleasantly, if he would mind going to the lobby and get her a cup of tea – decaf if they had it. Tyler smiled at her ... relieved that the mysterious dark cloud had lifted.

Five minutes later, he was back with two Styrofoam cups, topped with white plastic lids. He had gotten himself some decaf tea as well ... knowing it would please Annie if he drank with her. She was sitting in bed with her back against a pillow on the headboard. He gave her her tea, then sat in a high-backed chair in front of the curtained window to her right ... preferring to be in a chair for the inevitable ensuing conversation. He was sufficiently experienced with female rituals to remain silent and allow Annie to choose the words and tone to resume normal relations. He smiled at her and watched her. She took the lid from her tea, laid it on the lamp stand, and then brought the cup to her mouth. She jerked her head backwards, remarking at the heat of the tea. He was glad she didn't frown at him for not warning her. After they sipped at their teas for about five minutes in silence, Annie was ready to talk. He knew it would not begin with an apology.

"I think you're right, Ty. There's a good chance that we were abducted. Even though it would sound absolutely crazy to tell anyone – and we're not going to – it's about the only way to explain what happened. I think we have to accept the fact that those slimy creatures took us and did things to us. What I keep thinking about – over and over – is why us? Why did they pick *us* and what did they *do* to us? Were we just specimens to them ... like insects? Apparently, they aren't out to hurt us ... as far as we know. We're both in one piece with no bumps or bruises. That's the only thing that keeps me from screaming out loud. They're real things from some other planet ... but at least they're, apparently, harmless. But even though they don't mean us any harm ... I can't bear the thought of them coming to get us again. It makes me sick. And ... how dare they come into our house! Like we're just some lower form of life! How dare they! Maybe they just looked at us ... but I don't ever want to be touched by them again, Ty! Oh ... Ty ... they had me on that table with my legs spread and were ... I can't even say it. Oh God ... I feel like I'm going to throw up."

She put down her tea and ran to the bathroom. Tyler could see her on her knees with her head in the toilet, violently vomiting. He knew not to go to her. When it came to throwing up, she wanted no one near her and no one touching her. He walked to the bathroom and closed the door ... knowing she'd appreciate the privacy. The retching continued for quite a while. After it stopped he heard her gargling and spitting into the sink. She came out a short time later, looking very pale and weak. She climbed into bed, pulled the pillow onto the mattress and the blanket to her neck. She asked Tyler to turn off the light beside her side of the bed then rolled onto her right side, facing the center of the bed. A few minutes later she was asleep.

This never ceased to amaze Tyler. One minute she could be talking, then, like flipping a light switch, she would be asleep. He had never, in his entire life, gone to sleep so suddenly. He always had to undergo a slow transition from waking to sleeping ... often taking a half-hour or more. It always began with reading, so after Tyler showered, shaved, and brushed his teeth, he took off his clothes and got, naked, into bed, on his appointed left-hand side. He read the paper for about twenty minutes then became drowsy. After turning out the light, he quickly slipped into sound slumber.

CHAPTER 15

Upon awakening, Annie calmly suggested to Tyler that since they hadn't finished their conversation of the previous evening, they should get their breakfast in the lobby and bring it back to their room and talk while they ate. Tyler was agreeable to the suggestion ... both for eating in the room – which he liked – and for Annie's calm, regarding the discussion. He sincerely hoped it would hold this time.

With Annie eating on the bed and Tyler at the desk, Annie reignited their discussion.

"We really have to decide what to say to Dr. Dryden, Tyler. We have to call him before noon. Do we want to talk to him or not. What do you think?"

"No, no ... I want to hear from you, first."

"Why? I always like to hear from you, first."

"Now don't go getting all pissed off, Annie ... but usually when I go first, it starts an argument."

"Whatever, Tyler. OK ... if you insist ... I'll go first – just to make you happy."

Instead of starting, Annie remained silent. Tyler waited her out. She finally shook her head, looked at the ceiling and began.

"I'm really torn. I was awake all night thinking about it."

"You sure looked sound asleep to me."

"Well I wasn't. Anyway ... I'm really torn about it. It truly makes me sick to talk about it ... and if we talk about it, we're admitting to Dr. Dryden – and to ourselves – that we were actually abducted. Just talking about it last night made me vomit. So I don't know, physically, if I can do it. You said, last night, that you accept that we were probably abducted and seemed to fine with it ... so I suppose you wouldn't have any trouble talking to Dr. Dryden about it."

Annie stopped. Tyler knew this was a demand for a response that he could not defer.

"I could talk about it. I feel like I'm crazy even admitting it's a probability ... but I have to find a way to accept it. No sense trying to deny it. I think it's very likely what happened to us."

"Doesn't it make you sick?"

"Not sick. The more I think about it the more *angry* I get about it ... those fucking slime-balls coming into our house. I'm sleeping with a shotgun beside me from now on ... and if they ever come again, several of them aren't going back home to their slime-ball planet. As a matter of fact ... even though it's illegal in Nebraska, I'm sawing off my ten-gauge just for them. One shot and half of them go down."

"Oh Tyler. That scares me. I mean, they apparently don't want to hurt us ... but if you do that, they just might retaliate."

"I'll take my chances. No way am I gonna let either of us be a specimen again. Especially you. You didn't tell me what they did to you ... but you told me enough. Just think ... what would I do if some guy grabbed you and did that to you?"

"You'd kill him, Ty – I know you would. But honey ... these aren't regular people. Who knows what they're capable of."

"Look, honey ... let me be a man. Don't make me be a coward ... just because they're a bunch of big slimy frogs. I'm going to protect my family – regardless."

"OK, honey. I'm not going to argue with you. You have every right to protect us ... especially once we have the baby. As a matter of fact, if they'd try to touch my baby, I'd kill them myself."

"So what's it going to be, Annie? Do we see him or not?"

"Actually ... now that you've gotten me mad about this, I kind of feel different about it. You're right ... who do they think they are, coming into our house? I'm with you, Tyler. We fight. No one is going to get near my baby whether they're from Earth or any other place. I'll talk to the doctor and I'll tell him just how feel. To hell with those slimy creeps."

"Geez, Annie ... I've heard you curse twice in the last twenty-four hours. What's getting into you?"

"I think my mother's instinct is kicking in."

CHAPTER 16

At five-fifteen, Annie and Tyler sat down with Dr. Dryden in the same chairs they had chosen the day before. Dr. Dryden began.

"I want to know, first, what made you decide to come back?"

Annie answered.

"Tyler got me mad."

"What do you mean?"

"Tyler got me mad. I was all scared and emotional even thinking that those slimy creatures came into my house and touched me ... but Tyler told me he was angry about it. He said he was going to start sleeping with a shotgun and that he'd kill them if they tried to get us again. Then I started thinking what I'd do if they got near my baby ... and I realized that I'd kill them if they did. So ... I went from being scared to being mad. We've decided to defend ourselves, Doctor Dryden. That's what our great-grandparents did against the Indians that used to raid the farms around our area. They didn't run and hide ... they stood there and fought back. And I think about these slimy creatures the same way our ancestors thought about the Indians ... protecting your family from savages."

"That's very interesting. That's actually the first time I've heard that reaction about aliens. Let me ask you ... why would you want to kill these aliens? It's apparent they don't mean you any harm."

"That's what I said to Tyler at first ... but he made me realize that we have a right to keep them out of our house and to keep them from touching either of us – or the baby."

"But if they mean you no harm ... why do you want to cause them harm?"

Tyler jumped in.

"Hold on, Doc. Just what the hell are you saying? Are you telling me that we have to submit to these slime balls and let them come into our house and take us away and do what they want with us – and to our baby – just because they're from another planet? Are you kidding me?"

"I just question starting a war with these people. Who knows where that would lead?"

"What are you ... the intergalactic goodwill ambassador?"

"All right ... we don't have to get insulting about this."

"I'm not insulting you ... you're insulting me – suggesting that me protecting my family from house invaders is some kind of bad thing. I think you'd do better taking the position that no one has a right to break into anyone else's house and take them away ... whether they're from here or some other planet."

"OK ... I get your point. I've just never looked at it that way. Since I've never had any case of aliens doing any harm to anyone ... I always took the point of view that we should act the same way. What you're saying is that even if they don't do you any physical harm, they still have no right to come into your house and take you away."

"That's right."

'That's a valid point of view. I had just never thought of it that way. Of course ... if you're going to take this position ... you're going to have to take the risks that come with it. If you become violent ... they may do the same ... and all of you may end up dead – you, Annie, *and* the baby."

'That's the risk I'll have to take. That was the stakes my great-grandparents took."

"But with your great grand-parents, the Native Americans presented a risk to them."

"How do we know the aliens don't present a risk to us? I mean ... what the hell are they here for? What do they want?"

"I told you my suggestion ... that it's strictly exploration."

"But how do you know that's as far as it goes? What else might they have in mind?"

"I really don't know. I hadn't thought about it. Actually ... I have to take that back. I had some passing thoughts in your case."

Annie jumped in.

"What do you mean?"

"Well ... first I have a question."

"OK"

"You told me that you and Tyler thought you'd never have a baby."

"That's right."

"Did anyone ever tell you why you couldn't have a baby?"

"Yes ... we went to quite a few doctors to find out why I couldn't get pregnant."

"What did you find out?"

"They did a million tests and they all said I was infertile. Apparently, I have eggs, but there's something wrong with my uterus and I can't carry a baby. We thought about getting a surrogate ... you know ... some woman and we'd fertilize an egg of mine with Tyler's sperm and she'd carry it – you know what I mean. But we just didn't like the whole idea so we just resigned ourselves to not having a baby. But what's this got to do with our situation?"

"Well ... the only event that seems to be tied in with your having these nightmares is your pregnancy."

"So?"

"If we all agree that you two were abducted by aliens not from this planet ... then it begs the question as to the possible connection with a pregnancy occurring at around the same time."

Annie became very agitated. She raised her voice.

"What are you saying!!?"

"I'm just posing the question that, perhaps, there is a connection with your going from being completely infertile to being pregnant at the same time you were abducted by aliens."

Annie was on her feet.

"What are you trying to do to me?!! I have a baby growing inside of me! It's my baby ... it has absolutely nothing to do with those slimy creatures that took us away. Nothing!! Do you hear me!!!?

Annie burst into tears and Tyler jumped up and embraced her. At the same time, he spoke very sternly to Dr. Dryden.

"What are you doin, man? What the hell are you doin?"

Dr. Dryden stood up.

"I'm sorry ... I'm really sorry. It was just something I couldn't ignore. I'm sorry."

Annie spoke into Tyler's ear.

"Get me out of here, Tyler."

Tyler put his arm around Annie's shoulder and began leading her out of the room. He looked back at Dr. Dryden.

"We gotta go, Doc."

CHAPTER 17

As promised, Tyler sawed-off his ten-gauge shotgun and began putting it beside him in bed every night. If the aliens wanted to invade the McFarland household, they would be in for the fight of their lives. Annie stopped working at the bakery in her seventh month and stayed at home. After Tyler left for work, she kept the ten-gauge handy, which, as an experienced hunter, she could handle quite well. They told no one about their conclusion that they had been abducted. At times, they felt that, perhaps, they were overreacting ... but when they read in the paper about recent sightings of strange lights in the sky throughout Kansas and Nebraska, their commitment to their fortress was buoyed.

Annie watched for UFO programs with a new sense of urgency ... looking for insight as to how others were reacting to the phenomenon. Tyler was now watching with her. One show in particular caught her interest. She taped it for their continued perusal. It was about people who claimed to have been abducted by aliens. One segment featured their doctor – Dr. Dryden – conducting group therapy with ten alleged abductees. In the past, Annie would watch such programs with a sense of entertainment. Now, it was, for both her and Tyler, a study. The therapy group displayed a uniform sense of terror over their abductions. They all related experiences quite similar to the McFarland's ... the bedside encounter ... the examination room ... the tests. All had a profound fear of a possible return of the aliens. Several of them reported that they had been taken, on more than one occasion. One woman, in particular, Annie found very disturbing. She said she was pregnant and that the aliens took her, extracted the baby, and then told her that the baby was theirs. Annie simply did not allow herself to believe this woman. She couldn't.

As Tyler and Annie watched the program, they both talked to the TV, telling the members of the group to grow a spine and stand up to the alien creeps. Annie found herself swelling with pride over Tyler's courage and his willingness to protect his family. Yes ... the frog-like aliens had terrified him ... but he was willing to fight them. That was true courage – being afraid yet finding the strength to overcome your fear and standing up against it. That's what her granddad had told her about World War Two. He was only eighteen when he was on the boats, heading toward Normandy. He said he was so scared that he threw-up on the troop carrier. So did a lot of other guys. But he had done his job. He didn't quit and run. He charged off the landing craft and looked for Germans to kill. With men dying all around him, he had made his way to the cliffs and, later, fought with other brave, scared men ... all the way to Paris.

The men on the program struck her as total wimps ... relating their terror of the aliens with tears in their eyes. She would say to Tyler, "What's the matter with these guys?" Tyler's courage had given her courage – and the desire to fight back. If she didn't have someone like Tyler for a husband, she imagined she could be like one these frightened women on the show. It got her thinking about modern men in general. They sure weren't like her husband ... or like her dad or granddad. She had grown up with real men ... who could handle belligerent horses or stubborn cattle ... use a gun, and had been in their share of fistfights growing up. She had never lived in a city ... but the TV programs she watched about modern city men left her in disgust ... with their effeminate, timid behavior – the women often displaying more balls than their male friends. She had, on more than one occasion, remarked to Tyler that she hoped we would never have to fight another world war because she doubted there were enough real men left in America to fight it.

On June the 15th, she had their baby. They named her Cassandra, after her grandmother. With the birth of their daughter and her total immersion into motherhood and the associated commitment of time, love, and work ... she had almost totally forgotten about the alien problem. Tyler didn't. He slogged his way to his meaningless job every workday, then home see his devoted wife and precious daughter but never did he forget the potential threat to his family. The baby had redoubled his vigilance. Unable to sleep at times, he would walk around the house, gun in hand, searching for intruders.

CHAPTER 18

Gleed Trema addressed the crew of the Enverton in the Mission Training Room. He was an engineer and had been asked to explain the native 731 residential dwellings and how to gain entry. On a screen, he showed them a typical door found on a 731 residential structures.

"Most of the doors to 731 residential structures are of a very ancient design. In most cases they will be made of wood ... and, occasionally, metal. They require manual manipulation to open. "

He pointed to the door knob.

"You will need to grasp this round extension and turn it to your right to open the door. Turn it to your right then push ... and the door will open. There are, also, some doors that have a straight or slightly curved extension."

He displayed this type of door

"With these doors, you will need to press the extension downward then push the door forward. The natives frequently lock their doors ... particularly at night ... so you will need to know how to disable the locks they use."

He displayed a dead bolt apparatus on the screen.

"This is a common example of a 731 lock. The natives push a specially made piece of metal into this small slot in the lock to open it. Turning the metal piece causes this round cylinder to slide out of the locking hole and allows the door to open. There are, also, sometimes, locks on the extension piece."

He displayed such an extension.

"A piece of metal is also inserted into this small slot in the extension then turned. This allows the extension to turn and, thus, opens the door. Now ... we don't have the special metal piece for the particular locks you will encounter ... so to bypass these locking systems, simply remove them. You can quickly penetrate either wood or

metal with your beam knives, so simply cut out the upper
lock and remove it. Then try the extension. If it is also
locked, cut that out, as well. Before you try anything, of
course, check to see if the door is locked in the first place.
Natives who live in sparsely populated areas often leave
their doors unlocked, day and night. We will, of course, be
doing all our interventions at night for obvious reasons."

Trema put his hands on his hips and faced the crew.

"Any questions?"

Tunan Vidry, Enverton's Chief Engineer, spoke up.

"What do you suggest we do if we run into a
troublesome door we can't get open?"

"Don't force it. If you can't open it, easily ... use a
window."

"What's the recommended entry method on a window?"

Trema displayed a typical 731 window.

"Well ... as you can see, it's just thin glass and wood ...
sometimes glass and either metal or a polymer composite.
Either way ... it's easy to cut with your beam knives. Just
be careful you don't drop the cut-out. The glass will break
and make quite a racket. Also, keep in mind that their
windows will be a tight squeeze for Amburans to get
through, given our relative size – so doors are much
preferable for entrance."

Trema faced the crew with crossed arms.

"Anything else?"

With no further questions, he ceded the floor to Tenu
Van. The muscular special forces soldier strode to the
front of the room and put his hands on his hips.

"First ... if you have any questions while I'm talking,
speak up. Don't wait. All right ... one of my specialties is
native extractions. They can be very tricky. We'll work
with a team of five. I will be on every extraction crew along
with Captain Plegrue, Lieutenant Zuly, and two other
combat soldiers. The combat soldiers and I will do the
entry and lead the extraction crew to the subject. We will
have the responsibility to protect the Captain and his First
Mate."

Communications Chief Wenlen raised his hand.

"What sort of communications equipment will the crew
need?"

"All of us will need translation gear ... both broadcasting and receiving which, I assume, Chief, you will provide us. The base, here – as I understand it – has the soft wear for every language and dialect spoken on 731. We will need to understand everything a native may say and if we have to say something to a native, they will have to understand us. I'm sure you can fix us up with that sort of communications gear."

Wenlen nodded.

"Now ... many 731 natives keep weapons in their homes and these weapons are lethal. If we're not very careful ... we could lose crew members on this mission. Their weapons are ancient – but still deadly. They still use a combustible powder explosion to propel a metal projectile. Some of you may have seen this sort of weapon in our museums."

Van put a combustible powder rifle on the screen.

"I have actually fired one these ... and believe me ... it can put a big hole right through you. We are under orders to refrain from deadly force unless it becomes absolutely necessary ... so our weaponry will be set to stun. If that is insufficient, we will switch to kill mode. Our first line of defense, however, will be persuasion. If we are confronted by a hostile native, we will try to persuade the native to refrain from violence. I understand there will be a presentation by an anthropologist, this morning, on recommended communications methods with 731 natives."

Anjo Manzy, Combat Officer, spoke up.

"Have you ever done an extraction on 731 before, Captain Van?"

"No, I have not. To my knowledge, before this Olenreth action, there's never been an extraction on 731. Is that correct, Captain Plegrue?"

"That's right, Captain."

"First Mate Zuly will do all of the actual extractions. She will take physical possession of all targeted subjects. All the subjects will be native infants. The anthropologist, I was told, will also cover techniques on how to handle the 731 infants."

Tenu Van stopped and looked over the crew ... then gave his summary.

"Here's the short story. A good extraction will be one in which we make entry ... get the subject ... bring it back to our base, here ... they do whatever testing they need to do on it ... then we return the infant to its home ... and no one will know this ever happened. We're going to do twelve of these extractions ... let's hope all of them are a short story. Any other questions?"

None appearing, Dr. Vonly Rudden took the floor. She displayed an inappropriate, enormously stretched smile. Thanner Plegrue thought to himself that this was a classic female social scientist.

"Good morning, crew!"

Return greetings were issued in an unenthusiastic, bass tone, group murmur. Only Lieutenant Zuly was heard to actually return an energetic "Good Morning!" ... about which, she was promptly embarrassed and regretful.

"I'm very happy to speak with you today! I hope you're enjoying your stay on our base and find your accommodations to your liking!"

She paused ... but seeing absolutely no reaction to her solicitous comments, she proceeded, undaunted.

"Well ... OK. Let's talk about some things that could be helpful to you on your very important mission. First ... I was asked to comment on communicating with 731 natives. First, I must tell you ... other than the unfortunate intervention by the Olenreths ... no other sector crews have directly interacted with the 731 natives – so, everything I'm about to tell you is based strictly upon our studies of the natives. We have extensively examined their electronic communications, in particular ... we've intercepted their movies, their dramas, documentaries, news programs ... and we've read massive amounts of their written histories, novels, biographies, and a wide assortment of other miscellaneous materials. We've also listened to and analyzed their music and theatrical productions. Having done all of this ... we have developed a rather comprehensive assessment of the rational and emotional aspects of the natives ... as well as their habits, daily lives, social interactions, and family dynamics. I believe some of this may be helpful to you in achieving a successful mission."

She paused to look at her notes.

"All right ... let's begin with what you might expect upon entering a 731 dwelling. You will want to find the sleeping quarters of your extraction subject as soon as possible without awakening the parents of the subject. The natives have one, two, and, occasionally, three level dwellings. In nearly all instances, the sleeping rooms are placed in close proximity to one another. In dwellings of two or more floors, the sleeping rooms are nearly always on the second floor. Normally there are three or four sleeping rooms per dwelling. Unlike Amburans, whose families all sleep in the same room, the 731 native parents sleep separate from their offspring ... even when their offspring are infants. We suggest you do an interior scan before entering a dwelling to determine the whereabouts of the infant subject. 731 infants are quite small, compared to ours. Their birth weight is only about seven pounds or so – nothing like our twenty pound babies! They are only about twenty inches long ... which is, of course, much smaller than ours. So look for a very small image when searching for the subject."

Dr. Rudden stopped and, again, mechanically spread the hyperbolic smile across her face.

"Are there any questions so far?"

Vinta Zuly raised her hand and was acknowledged.

"What sort of sleeping container do the natives use for their infants? Are they covered containers like Amburans use?"

"No ... they are open to the ambient air. The 731 natives seem to not mind their young breathing the ambient air during sleep, as odd as that may sound. The container looks somewhat like a cage ... with narrow, wooden bars on all sides of the container – they're about two feet in height so you will need to lift the subject from the bottom of the container to extract it. I should have an image of one but I couldn't locate it for this presentation. Now, from our studies, we have found that 731 infants eat very frequently ... in small amounts. During their first months of life, they may eat every three hours. The infants have very small stomachs, obviously. Keep this in mind because the female parent will normally come to the subject's sleeping room and extract the subject to feed it on a rather frequent basis during the night. You may want to watch for this on your scan and plan for entry right after a feeding. Another thing ... the 731 infants can be easily awakened and when they are startled, they emit an enormous amount of sound from their mouths. It's similar to the shrieks of a bandoo ... if you've ever heard one in a zoo at home. It's truly astounding, the volume of noise their infants are capable of creating. Anyway ... be prepared for this when you extract the subject. I would have a tranquilizing rod on hand to deal with this. You may want to consider using the wand before the extraction ... just to make sure the subject remains asleep."

Vinta raised her hand, again.

"Is that safe ... I mean for the baby?"

"We think so ... from the testing we've done on lower 731 species that have similar physiologies to the natives. But we can't say for sure, however ... since we've never done any such testing on a native infant. There's always a risk, so use your own judgment when it come to tranquilizing. It wouldn't work to end up with a dead subject, would it? You may want to try a manual tranquilizing method if you're wary about using the wand. I brought one of these devices with me."

Dr. Rudden reached into the container she had placed on the table, and pulled out a pacifier.

"This odd-looking device is used – with great success – by 731 parents, to calm their infants. We're not exactly sure why it works – it doesn't deliver any nourishment – but they insert this device into the mouth of a crying infant and it causes the infant to become calm and quiet. I'm very glad we don't have to deal with such noisy babies on Ambura, aren't you?"

Dr. Rudden laughed at her own comment. She was the only one in the room who did. Vinta took quiet umbrage to the comment ... wishing she had the chance to experience an Amburan baby – not caring if it were quiet or not. Dr. Rudden went on, undeterred.

"Like our infants, 731 infant offspring can also be calmed by close body contact with them ... embracing them and rubbing their backs and heads. Bouncing motions and quiet humming to them is good, also. In general ... you can handle their infants very much as you would handle one of ours."

"Is there anything else you want to know about the 731 infants?"

Vinta raised her hand.

"Well, Lieutenant Zuly ... you are very inquisitive today."

Vinta did not return the doctor's disingenuous smile but went right into her question.

"When our surgeons do their testing on these babies, will they anesthetize them first?"

"Well, Lieutenant, I don't really know. That's a rather odd question, isn't it?"

Vinta Zuly took visible umbrage at Dr. Rudden condescension.

"Listen, doctor ... I resent your impertinent tone! I'm the one who is responsible for extracting every one of these 731 infants – and if I have a question ... it's your job to answer it – not to make commentary of the nature of the question. You may not be a member of the military ... but you're being paid by the military and I'll have none of your disrespect!"

Thanner Plegrue smiled to himself – pleased to see Lieutenant Zuly assert herself in front of the crew and put this haughty ass of a doctor in her place. The rest of the crew openly smiled. The doctor was nonplussed. Finally finding her voice and struggling to regain her composure, she responded in a shaken voice.

"I apologize, Lieutenant Zuly, if you took offense at my comment. I intended none, I'm sure. As for your question ... the surgeons, I'm aware, don't always use anesthetics on lower-life species to do testing ... so I can't really answer your question for certain."

"So, they might do invasive testing on a baby without anesthesia?"

"Yes ... that's possible – but it's not an Amburan, Lieutenant. These are primitive creatures."

"How would you like them to do invasive testing on you without anesthetics, doctor?"

Thanner Plegrue quickly intervened.

"OK ... let's move this along, doctor. You're supposed to brief us on communicating with the adult natives – so let's get to it."

"Yes ... well, OK ... let's talk about that. If you encounter a situation where you have to confront an adult native ... there are some things you need to know. These 731 adults are quite emotional. The males can be very violent and are easily provoked. The females cry easily – but in cases in which they sense their infant is in danger, they, too, can be quite violent, as well. Captain Van explained their weapons ... I can tell you about their propensities. The adult native uses its weapons quite readily ... and will willingly kill anyone who presents a threat to itself or to a member of its tribe. You must be ready for this. They are far more likely to resort to violence than any Amburan would. Even if you disarm the adult male, he can still be very dangerous. He will use anything he can grab, as a weapon, and can inflict quite a bit of bodily damage simply by using his own body. These 731 natives have developed quite an art form of inflicting injury by use of their own body parts, alone, particularly their arms and legs. They also – if you can believe this – use their heads to inflict severe damage on an opponent. Such a use of one's head, as they employ, would shatter an Amburan's skull. Of course, their skulls are much thicker than ours. Even the females are quite capable of violence – if sufficiently provoked. They tend to use their teeth and nails – like some of our wild species on Ambura – when they go on the attack. So ... caution is the word with the adult natives. They're an extremely dangerous species."

Benur Iler posed a question.

"Is there any way to reason with this species?"

"If you can calm them, some of the natives have the intelligence to be reasonable. You can try. If I were you, I'd try to make them understand that you don't present a danger to them – or to their infant offspring. Tell them that there are necessary tests that you must perform on their offspring, that will do it no harm and that it is for its own benefit. Of course ... don't mention *anything* about the ultimate elimination of their offspring if it turns out to be an Olenreth mutant. No telling what they may do if they discovered this eventuality."

Vinta Zuly jumped in.

"So, what you're saying is, is that we have to lie to these natives about what we intend to do to their babies?"

"Well, of course. These are a very violent species. We can't afford to, knowingly, provoke them. It would be too dangerous for us. They are quite capable of killing your crew members, Lieutenant Zuly."

"I'm well aware of the dangers to my crew, doctor. I'm simply not comfortable with intentionally deceiving the natives."

"I guess you and I just have a different view of this species, Lieutenant. You are looking at them as though they were Amburans or some other advanced species ... I don't look at them in that way. I'm an anthropologist and, as such, I make an objective judgment of the species I encounter. I refrain from projecting advanced species characteristics onto them. It's a common thing that many do – but as scientists, or soldiers, we must resist this temptation for our own good. The 731 natives, in my opinion, are not very highly evolved in the grand scheme of things, and I put them at a much lower level on the evolutionary scale, than the inhabitants of the advanced sectors."

"Like the Olenreths?"

Dr. Rudden allowed a flash of anger to creep into her expression.

"The Olenreths are highly advanced as a species ... they simply don't conform to some of the norms expected among the other sectors."

"So you're an Olenreth supporter?"

"I did not say that, Lieutenant!! I am simply saying that, despite their problems, they are much further evolved than the 731 natives."

Vinta glared at Dr. Rudden but remained silent. It was apparent that Dr. Rudden had had enough of the briefing. She rapidly delivered her final words to the crew of the Enverton, devoid of her initial, hyperbolic enthusiasm.

"If there's nothing more, that's the extent of my briefing."

She quickly gathered together her materials and hurried out of the room.

CHAPTER 19

Two days after the briefing, the extractions began. Thanner Plegrue, Vinta Zuly, Tenu Van, Benur Iler, and Anjo Manzy comprised the team. Thanner was very pleased. Not only did he have a distinguished Special Forces Officer with him but his best friend, Benur, as well – a brave and experienced combat veteran – and Anjo ... also a valiant and seasoned fighter. Given the mission of extracting infant subjects, he was also pleased to have a female on his crew ... and silently took back all of the complaining he had done about a female on a combat mission. Perhaps, he thought, the Sector Command knew what they were doing after all. Given the composition of his team, if they were to have a successful mission, this would give them their best chance. It was decided that they would attempt only one extraction per night. Just after sunset, the team knelt on the boarding ramp in front of their small scout ship as an Amburan Base priest administered a blessing upon them.

Vinta Zuly was nervous to the point of nausea. She hoped she would be up to the task before her ... and prayed they would be spared any confrontations with the natives. Her greatest fear was that she would not be able to keep her emotions in check when the time came to take a sleeping baby from the love, care, and protection of its parents – and deliver it into the hands of cold-hearted surgeons for testing. That they may proceed without anesthesia, she fought a losing battle to avoid contemplation. These thoughts kept her awake the entire night before they deployed ... and denied her any semblance of an appetite.

They were equipped with their communication devices and atmosphere converters. The converters were implanted into the crew's nostrils by the base surgeons.

Once implanted, there was no physical sensation of their presence and they were quite efficient at converting the ambient atmosphere into the necessary hydrogen-heavy mixture required by Amburans. The surgeons also implanted a receiving translator into the right ear of each crew member, to reconfigure native speech to Amburan. Speech modifiers were implanted in the back of their throats. All crew members had a small device attached to their left wrists, to turn these devices on or off.

The combat team members were equipped with an assortment of weapons. Each would carry a neutron rifle on the extraction, which could be slung over their shoulders when they needed use of their hands. They also carried a small neutron handgun and a beam sword on their weapons belt. As instructed, the rifle and handgun were set at stun mode. Lieutenant Vinta and Captain Plegrue also had neutron handguns on their belts. In Vinta Zuly's equipment pack were two pacifiers and a medical wand to render the infant unconscious if necessary. Being a very religious person, she also wore necklace with a medallion bearing the image of Annah.

Minveer Reg, Enverton's First Pilot, was assigned to this mission but was not on the extraction team and would remain with the ship during the extraction. His mission flight plan arranged the extractions by geographical groupings. The twelve extractions were in groups of four with three extractions per group. It was decided to begin with the group closest to the underwater base.

Lieutenant Reg conducted all of the preflight checks then steered the scout ship through the portal and into the black depths of the ocean. This being considered a clandestine mission, he ran without the aid of lights, using sonar, instead, to avoid collisions with other ships or sea creatures. Upon reaching the surface, he took the ship to altitude and inputted the coordinates of the first extraction site. In an instant, they were hovering above the targeted native dwelling. He turned on the ship's night vision and examined the layout of the landscape below. It was a very sparsely populated area with no other native dwelling for miles around the site. There was very little vegetative growth around the dwelling – other than several large trees, very close to the dwelling. Reg selected a landing site and slowly descended toward the surface, extending the landing gear just before contact.

Having landed, Reg asked Captain Plegrue if he should lower the ramp. Plegrue told him to wait a few minutes. His team was still seated and they all turned to look at him. None of them wore anything except thin, form-fitting, dark blue uniforms and gray shoes made of a soft material – no helmets or any other equipment except their weapons belts. If they encountered a native, they wanted to look as non-threatening as possible, and other than their extreme height and unusual hair, they looked rather benign. Plegrue addressed his team.

"Let's make this a good mission. Get in and get out. Remember our orders. We do no harm to the natives unless absolutely necessary. Keep your talking to an absolute minimum and use hand signals as often as possible. Let's put on our night glasses right now."

The team members opened their equipment packs, took out their glasses and put them on.

"Everyone touch your lens and make sure your glasses are working."

Each person put a finger to the lens to ensure their night vision was functioning. All were.

"All right, then ... check your weapons."

The team went through a check of all their weapons and all gauges indicated they were properly functioning.

"When we get outside, check your monitors to see if your atmosphere converters are working properly. I don't want anyone going unconscious on me. Everyone turn on their speech and receiver translators and let's make sure they're working."

All pushed the two communications buttons on the small control band attached to their left wrist.

"OK ... one at a time, say something. First Mate ... you go first. I'll turn off my receiver translator to check you out."

Vinta recited the lines of her favorite poem. Thanner heard her words in what he recognized as the 731 language for this designated landing site that was played for them in their language briefing before the mission.

"Good. You're OK."

Plegrue conducted the same test for each of his crew members. When it came time to test his speech converter, he turned it on and had Vinta turn her receiver off. It worked. They then checked their receivers by reversing the process.

"Let's go and let's do it."

He got up from his seat and the team did likewise. Plegrue addressed the pilot.

"Open the ramp, Lieutenant Reg."

"Opening ramp. Sir."

Two sections of the ship immediately parted – one upward, the other downward. Captain Plegrue walked across the departure area and descended the ramp with his extraction crew behind him. All on the surface, he spoke to Reg via his transmitter.

"Close her up, Mr. Reg."

The two open sections immediately came together, sealing the ship.

Thanner address the team.

"Check your monitors. Is everyone's atmosphere converter working?"

The team members checked and all converters were working properly.

"Let's go."

Tenu Van took the lead with Iler and Manzy ... Plegrue and Zuly following. The combat soldiers had their rifles in ready position. Everyone could feel the heavy gravity pushing down on their bodies. When they got to within about a hundred yards of the house, Plegrue stopped the team and pulled out his scanner. He scanned the house and found the natives still moving about the dwelling. He reported his finding.

"Oh shit ... they're still up and about. We must be here too early. Why the hell didn't they tell us when these natives go to bed? Well ... everyone just sit down and we'll wait."

As they sat, they studied the sky with interest. The stars were considerably smaller and fewer than an Amburan night sky. They noticed that with so few stars, there seemed to be patterns among them, and they pointed out various configurations to one another as they found them. Every fifteen minutes or so, Thanner Plegrue scanned the dwelling for movement. As Vinta Zuly sat there, she was experiencing a sense that she wasn't getting enough air to breathe. She quietly informed Tanner of this. He told her to let him see her monitor. It indicated that her system was adequately aerated and expressed his opinion that it was either the effect of the heightened gravity or that she was suffering from anxiety. He told her that either way, she was perfectly fine physically ... and that she probably just needed to calm down.

The night was quite warm, with a balmy breeze blowing from the southwest. The silence was occasionally interrupted by the sounds emitted by some animal species. Focusing on the soft breeze caressing her face, Vinta Zuly felt herself calming, and her breathing came easier. She thought of the adult couple inside, safely sleeping in this beautiful breeze. They had, no doubt, fallen in love and had rejoiced at the birth of their baby. The fact that they would live such short lives made every moment of their life all the more poignant and precious. When something is fleeting, love and beauty must be cherished. She tried to picture herself as the female adult ... asleep beside the male she loved and near to the baby that had grown inside her. Her heart literally ached as she thought of these things. If it were possible, she would trade places with the female inside the dwelling in an instant ... even with all of the pain and suffering that came with short lives filled with sickness and the grief of death. At least they had passion – something that seemed to have been extinguished on Ambura. Yes ... she could live, disease-free, for hundreds – or thousands – of years to come ... but to what point? The thought of this infinite life became oppressive to her and she felt as though she might start screaming. She shook her head and halted her stream of thought. Thanner's voice brought her back to the task at hand.

"All right ... there's been no movement for forty-five minutes. Both the adults and the infant are in their beds and their respiration indicates slumber for all of them. Let's go."

They all stood up and in the same order of procession, advanced the hundred yards to the dwelling. As they passed in front of the house, they noticed that all of the windows were open and in the opened area was a very thin, wire mesh. Seeing this, Thanner considered using a window for entry but then decided against it because of the height of the window from the surface and the reduced space for ingress and egress – particularly with Vinta carrying an infant. They proceeded to a set of old wooden steps that led to a porch ... then across the porch to the door. They discovered there were two doors – not one, as the experts had represented. The interior door, made of wood, was open, and the exterior door, made of metal, was closed and was covered with the same fine, metal mesh as were the open window coverings.

Tenu Van looked at Thanner. He made hand motions for Tenu to try the door. He grabbed the small metal apparatus attached to the door and gently pulled it. The door moved slightly but was apparently locked in some fashion. Tenu put his face to the metal mesh and looked inside as he gently pulled on the door several times. He took out his beam knife, activated it, then cut a small section from the mesh about five feet from the floor of the porch and at the far right of the door. After removing the small section, he put his hand into the hole and felt around ... finding a very small locking mechanism. With a flip of his finger, the door was unlocked. Van turned to look at Thanner. He nodded and Van slowly opened the door. Vinta felt her heart jump and her breathing become a pant.

Tenu Van ducked his head under the door frame and gently placed his right foot on the old, wooden plank floor of the entryway. He pushed off of his left foot and stood on his right foot then brought his left foot up onto the floor. He took several cautious steps forward then motioned the rest of the team to follow. With ducked heads, they traversed the doorway then entered the house as quietly as their huge torsos would allow. When the entire team was indoors, they formed a tight circle. The tops of their heads touched the ceiling. There were rooms immediately to their left and right and a steep staircase ahead of them to their left. To the right of the staircase was a long hallway, leading to another room. Thanner Plegrue pointed toward the top of the staircase and Van nodded. Van placed his huge foot on the bottom riser and slowly shifted his weight onto the step. As he did, the compressed wood emitted a loud creaking noise. He immediately withdrew his foot and looked at Thanner. Thanner leaned his head toward Tenu Van and whispered in his ear.

"Try different parts of the step."

Tenu nodded. He turned toward the staircase and placed his right foot at the extreme right edge of the riser then began shifting his weight onto that foot. There was no sound so he continued the shift until he was standing on the first riser with all of his weight on his right foot. He slowly raised his left foot and placed it on the extreme left of the riser then cautiously shifted his weight until there was equal balance between the two. No sound. Van turned toward the group and made a motion with his left hand, signaling them to wait where they were. He turned toward the stairway and began the painstaking process of repeating the pattern he had used on the first riser. After several minutes, he reached the top of the stairs, then turned to motion the next team member to repeat his path. It was nearly fifteen minutes before the entire team was at the landing at the top of the stairs. From the dwelling scans, Thanner knew the whereabouts of the infant, and he motioned the direction to Van. At the first room on the right, Thanner grabbed Van's right elbow and pointed into the room. Van held up his hand for the rest of the team to remain where they were. He peered into the room, then took a cautious step across the threshold, ducking under the door frame as he did. Tenu Van took six steps to reach the infant's crib – against the wall to the right of the doorway. He motioned the rest to proceed. The team assembled around the crib and peered down at the sleeping infant. She was sleeping on her stomach with her head turned to her left. A soft white blanket covered her to her neck.

Vinta Zuly's heart swelled within her. The baby was tiny and her profile was heavenly and sweet. A sob began to emerge from her throat. The sound she made was detected by Thanner and his head swung in her direction, understanding what the sound meant. He looked into her eyes. She was struggling. Thanner leaned to her ear and whispered.

"Can you do this?"

She stared at him with wide eyes but finally closed them for a moment then nodded in the affirmative. Thanner motioned for the defense trio to guard the door. They moved to the center of the room and swung their rifles into firing position. Vinta Zuly studied the baby ... trying to decide how best to lift her. She reached down and gently grabbed the top edges of the blanket then, very slowly, began pulling it toward the baby's feet, eventually uncovering the baby. She was wearing a garment that entirely enclosed her, except for her head and hands. Vinta slid her left hand under the baby's chest and began to slowly lift her. The infant's head dropped onto the mattress as she did this. Vinta immediately lowered her back onto the mattress ... realizing that, apparently, unlike Amburan infants, 731 babies had very weak necks and were unable to support their heads. She then slipped her left hand under the infant's head and her right hand under the center of the baby's body. With this grip, she lifted the baby above the level of the crib's top rung ... then moved her to her own body ... laying the infant's head against her chest. She kept her left hand behind the infant's head and her right hand supported the baby's bottom.

Vinta's hands were so large that the baby was nearly invisible in her grip. She was stunned at the small size of the infant. Amburan infants were, at least, three times her size ... and she weighed so little, Vinta had almost no sensation of actually carrying anything. Vinta, instinctively, began swaying with the baby. She whispered to Thanner.

"I forgot to get out the sleep inducer. It's in my bag. Get it for me – just in case."

Thanner opened the bag and pulled it out. Vinta whispered again.

"You hold it for me."

Thanner nodded.

Vinta had a strong impulse to just stand there and sway with the baby, forever. She pretended it was hers. Thanner – seeing that she, apparently, had no inclination to get moving – whispered.

"We need to go, Vinta."

Vinta nodded and started toward the door. The baby made some tiny noises and Vinta rubbed her back, immediately quieting her. Seeing Vinta coming their way, the defense team moved toward the door, ahead of her and Thanner. Tenu Van went into the hallway and stopped to reconnoiter in both directions then started to slowly make his way toward the top of the staircase with the rest following. As he neared the top of the staircase, he heard a coughing sound – obviously coming from an adult – in the room directly in front of him, just past the staircase. He stopped instantly and held up his hand. After waiting ten seconds or so – without hearing any more sound emanating from the room – he stepped to the open door of the room and peered inside. There were two adults in a bed. The male was on the right side. He suddenly made a move ... rolling from his left side to his right side. Van instantly stepped to his right, out of the doorway, where he could not be seen by the male native. The rest of the team, in the hallway behind him, froze and held their collective breath.

After a full minute of frozen silence, Tenu Van carefully leaned toward the doorway and looked into the room. The man was motionless and snoring in fits and starts. He motioned for the team to move as he quietly placed his right foot at the extreme right of the top step then shifted his weight onto it. Using the same step strategy as he employed in his ascent, Van made his way to the bottom of the steps. One at a time, the team members traversed the staircase. Vinta Zuly was the first person to come down the steps after Van ... the team wanting to protect her from front and back. Once assembled at the bottom of the stairs, Thanner motioned for Tenu Van to begin the exit from the house. He slowly pushed open the screen door and held it for the remainder of the team to exit and cross the porch. He gently allowed the spring-attached screen door to close without a sound and made his way across the porch and onto the lawn where the team was waiting.

They knew they had to hurry. They needed to take the infant back to the base, allow time for the surgeons to do their testing, then get the baby back into its crib before the mother discovered it missing. While there would be no crying to awaken the mother for a feeding, it was possible the mother could awaken on her own and check on her baby. This could set off a series of untenable events if not contained, so Thanner had the three soldiers remain at the house while he and Vinta took the infant to the base. He ordered the combat team to immediately stun both adults if they heard any sounds of alarm coming from the house. Then – if the adults showed any signs of recovering from the stunning – use the anesthetic wand to keep them unconscious until the infant was returned to her crib. The combat team was also ordered to place both adults back into their bed after the stunning. Both the stunning and the anesthetic induced a degree of amnesia and the hope was that the couple would simply awaken in their beds with no memory of what had happened ... or, perhaps, think it was simply a bad dream. The combat team took up their vigil, sitting on the porch to the right of the door, leaning against the rough wooden siding of the house ... their rifles ready for action.

Thanner and Vinta rushed with the infant back to the ship, and arrived at the base within ten minutes after lift-off ... most of the time consumed in the lights-off descent through the water to the base. A transport was awaiting them at the docking ramp and, five minutes later, they were entering the base's medical facility. They took the lift to the third floor and rushed the baby to the surgeons awaiting them. A nurse took the baby from Vinta and hurried into the surgical suite.

Vinta resisted, for a moment, the nurse taking the baby from her arms. This was the longest period of time she had ever held an infant and had, almost instantly, formed an attachment to it ... engendering the sense of protectiveness that comes with it. Two minutes after the nurse had taken the infant to the surgeons, she heard a piercing shriek of pain coming from the suite. She instinctively jumped to her feet and sprang toward the surgery door. Thanner was barely able to grab her before she dashed into the suite. He tightly wrapped his arms around her body, restraining both of her arms. She violently resisted, twisting her head and body, writhing like a trapped animal ... kicking her legs wildly. Thanner shouted at her.

"Vinta!!! Stop!!! Stop!!!"

She screamed back at him.

"They're hurting my baby!!! Let me go you bastard!!!"

Her screaming made her even more uncontrollable, and her wild movement knocked the two of them onto the hospital floor. It turned into a wrestling match between them. Thanner couldn't believe the strength her frenzy had produced. It took all of his power to maintain control of her. Finally, Thanner lay on top of her and pinned her arms against the cold floor. She whipped her head left and right, screaming at him to get off of her. The commotion attracted several of the hospital workers. They rushed to the struggling pair and stared at Thanner with wide eyes ... wondering what Thanner wanted them to do. He looked up and shouted.

"Sedative!! Sedative!!"

A male worker pulled a wand from his pocket, quickly set the mode, then pressed tip of the wand to Vinta's temple. She was instantly asleep. Thanner released Vinta's arms and raised himself to a position of having one knee on each side of Vinta's body. A female attendant caught Thanner's eye and pointed to his mouth.

"You're bleeding, Captain."

Thanner wiped his mouth with the back of his right hand and saw it was covered with his dark yellow blood. The attendant reached toward him but Thanner shook his head.

"It's OK. Don't worry about it."

The male who had used the wand on Vinta disappeared and a minute later was back with a floating gurney. Thanner got off of Vinta and the three attendants placed her onto the gurney. Thanner addressed the trio.

"Put her in a room and keep her there."

They nodded and quickly moved down the hallway, pushing the gurney, then disappeared around a corner to their left. Thanner stood up and began pacing in disbelief as to what had just transpired. He was still breathing violently. While he was still pacing, the nurse came through the door with the baby. She handed it to Thanner and asked if everything was OK. He simply nodded, then turned and hurried back to the transport waiting outside the building, then back to the scout ship. Inside the ship, Minveer Reg asked him where Lieutenant Zuly was. Thanner shook his head.

"She's staying here."

In ten minutes time, they were back at the house. Thanner hurried to the porch to find the combat unit still leaning against the wall. He quietly climbed the porch steps, walked over to them and whispered.

"Anything going on?"

All three shook their heads in the negative. He whispered again.

"Then let's go."

They repeated their previous entry and put the infant back in her crib without incident then made an uneventful egress. Back in the scout ship, they all sat down and breathed a sigh of relief. Even though they had no confrontation with a native, the tension took its toll on the team. Thanner displayed a weary smile and spoke to the crew."

"Good job, guys. That was really good work."

Iler asked him where Vinta was.

Thanner said he'd tell him about it later.

CHAPTER 20

As soon as Thanner Plegrue returned to the Amburan Base from his mission, he went directly to the base hospital to see Vinta Zuly. There was a guard outside her door. Thanner nodded to him as he walked by, stiffly, into the room. He pressed the button to the left of the door to close it then walked in hard steps to the side of Vinta's bed. She was sitting up, leaning against a pillow, still in uniform. Vinta studied his face as he approached. It was not friendly. When he arrived at bedside, she noticed his lip had been cut. She inquired.

"What happened to your lip, Captain?"

"You really want to know?"

She looked puzzled.

"Yes ... of course."

"Well ... when you had your little fit outside the surgical suite, you split my lip with the back of your head."

Vinta's mouth dropped open.

"Oh, Thanner ... I'm really sorry."

"I'll live ... but my lip isn't the issue, is it?"

Vinta looked down into her lap and spoke very quietly.

"No."

"Look at me, Vinta."

She did.

"I can't have this on my crew. Your conduct was totally unacceptable as an officer of the Space Service. Do you realize I could have you court marshaled?"

She shook her head up and down.

"Yes."

"Can you give me any good reason I should not?"

"No."

"Explain to me what happened."

"I think you already know. I held my emotions in check for the entire extraction ... but when I heard that baby scream, I knew they were operating on her without any anesthesia. That's barbaric ... and I couldn't tolerate it. They had no right to inflict pain on that innocent, helpless baby when they could have easily used anesthesia."

"It made me angry when I heard it too ... but that's no excuse for you to go into a lunatic rage."

"All I can say about that is that you're not a woman who is at her genetic peak of wanting a baby. Court marshal me if you like ... but you simply have no idea what it's like to be a female. As sophisticated as we Amburans like to think we are ... nothing has really changed inside us. We still have all of our instincts that our brilliant scientists don't stop to think about. They provide us with our Fenzen and think that that solves everything. They're idiots. It doesn't solve anything ... it just makes us live forever. So here I am ... an Amburan woman who – like every Amburan woman before her – is driven by nature to have a baby. You wouldn't understand – but that's the way it is. Males have strong desires for lots of other things – besides sex – like adventure, sports, inventing, building, business ... lots of things. Women are made to want babies. And raise babies. We all like to say we're beyond that ... but it's a lie. Your generation was the last one that was allowed to be normal. Your women had their babies. Your wife had hers. If I'd get pregnant, they'd abort me and put me in prison for five years. They simply tell me I can't have a baby ... as though that solves everything."

Thanner was about to say something, but Vinta went on.

"When I held that native baby in my arms – especially after we left the dwelling and I was all she had for warmth and protection – I became her mother until I had her back in her own bed. I was responsible for her ... to see that no one hurt her. And when I heard those cold-hearted surgeons digging into her ... as though she was some kind of animal ... I had to do something. I couldn't stop myself. She was my baby and I had to protect her. That's it. I had to protect her."

Thanner went silent and was visibly thoughtful for a period of time.

"Believe it or not, Vinta ... I understand you. How you feel. How you felt. Like most men ... I've never really thought, much, about how women think. We want sex ... and that's about it. We don't have this insatiable urge to have a baby. I mean ... we're really happy when our wives have a baby ... but we don't have that overwhelming drive to have one. If a woman's need to have baby is like a guy's sex drive ... then that's something a guy could understand."

"I'm not a male ... but I think a man's need for sex is nothing compared to a woman's need to have a baby. You can solve your problem in a few minutes. We women live for years with our need."

"I suppose if I felt the way you did about that native infant ... I would have probably reacted the same way as you did when they hurt it. By the way ... you keep referring to the baby as a 'her' ... how do you know? It was completely covered with that sleep outfit."

"Oh please, Thanner. She was lying, tight against my chest. You don't think I can feel what kind of equipment she has – or doesn't have?"

Thanner shrugged his shoulders.

"I suppose ... but I don't think I would have noticed."

"Oh ... that's so surprising, Mr. Male."

Thanner laughed – and so did Vinta.

They both went silent ... an easy silence.

Finally a serious look came across Thanner's face.

"Look, Vinta ... I said I understood ... but I have a mission to run. I can't have this happening – ever again."

"I know that, Thanner. I'll tell you what ... I would have been OK if it hadn't been for their hurting the baby. I simply can't tolerate it. If I heard them doing that again ... I'd do the same thing. So ... how about this ... either you can take the baby from me ... and carry it into the hospital, yourself ... or you could talk to the surgeons and ask them to please use an anesthetic. How about that?"

Thanner thought about it then answered.

"That's reasonable. Do you have a preference?"

"Yes. It's strictly selfish. I want to have the baby in my arms as much as possible ... so I'd prefer you speak with the surgeons. Besides ... I could sleep better knowing they aren't going to make the babies undergo such pain."

"To tell you the truth, Vinta ... It bothers me, too. No reason they should be operating on an infant without anesthesia. I agree with you that just because they think of these natives as lower life forms, doesn't give them the right to be cruel to them ... especially these tiny infants."

Vinta gave Thanner a smile that was tinged with love. Thanner noticed. She spoke to him with words of the same color.

"You have a good heart, Thanner Plegrue."

Thanner felt himself blush. He couldn't believe it – and was embarrassed. He smiled shyly and said goodbye. He quickly left Vinta's room and went directly to see the head of surgery. He explained the situation and, shielding his First Mate, told the head surgeon that his objection to the lack of anesthesia was a result of how *he* felt about inflicting unnecessary pain on these infants. The head surgeon responded that, despite the fact that it was common practice to dispense with anesthesia on lower life forms, he would honor the Captain's request to use anesthesia and pass the order along to his staff. Thanner thanked him and hurried back to Vinta's room to deliver the news.

CHAPTER 21

The extractions progressed smoothly with the exception of a few incidents. On three occasions, they discovered the infant sleeping in the same room with the parents. Knowing it would be next to impossible to do the extraction without an encounter with the parents, they elected to simply anesthetize both adults before beginning the extraction. On the fifth extraction, the team was surprised by the mother, who had awakened and was coming down the hall toward the nursery. Van Tenu fired on her with stun mode. Fearing to awaken the male, if they returned her to the bed, they simply left her, there, lying in the hallway. On the seventh extraction, as the team was walking down the hallway toward the infant's room, the male apparently heard them, sprang from his bed and ran down the hallway, jumping on the trailing member of the team – Thanner Plegrue. Vinta Zuly, immediately preceding Thanner, heard and felt the commotion and dove on the much-smaller male native ... pulling him off of Thanner's back. She held him down on the carpet. Benur Iler pulled his wand from his belt and shouted to Vinta to hold his head steady. She placed a hand on each side of his head as Benur touched the wand to his left temple. The male adult was immediately unconscious, but the struggle had awakened the female, who sat up in the bed and began screaming. Benur instantly rotated in her direction and shot her with his rifle. The team carried the unconscious male back to the bed, covered them with their blanket, and went back to the extraction.

During the tenth extraction, as the team was descending the steps with the infant in hand, the female appeared at the top of the steps and began screaming. The male awakened and pushed past her and dove down the stairs, landing on the top of the last of the three team members still on the steps – Thanner, Vinta, and Benur. Thanner fell forward on top of Vinta – holding the baby – who, in turn, fell onto Benur. The four of them crashed into Anjo Manzy and Tenu Van, standing on the landing at the bottom of the steps. The native male thrashed furiously within the pile of bodies. Vinta closed her body around the infant, trying to protect it. Tenu Van finally put the native male into a choke hold and held on until he went unconscious. At this point, the female came charging down the stairs, screaming at the team to give her her baby. Anjo Manzy tackled her and she fell backwards, against the steps. He tried to calm her by assuring her her baby was completely safe and that they would do it no harm. This had no effect and she continued screaming and thrashing. With this, Anjo used his anesthetic wand on her. They carried the couple to their bed and covered them. For safety sake, Tenu Van used his wand on the male. The infant was unharmed in the ruckus.

This night, they were doing their final extraction – and were glad it was the last.

CHAPTER 22

On July 30th Tyler and Annie McFarland took little Cassie to the pediatrician for her six-week checkup. Everything was fine, except, according to Dr. Patterson, Cassie appeared, to her, to look a bit jaundiced. She told them there probably nothing to worry about but suggested a blood test to make sure. She gave them an order for the test and the McFarlands took the baby directly to the hospital for the blood draw. Tyler told Annie he couldn't watch them take blood from Cassie, so Annie went into the small room with Cassie when their number was called. The phlebotomist was a rather hefty male with a full beard and Annie came close to asking for someone else until he smiled at her and asked her if this was the first blood draw for the baby. She responded that it was and he told her he'd make sure it was as quick and as painless as possible.

He tied off Cassie's tiny arm with a very small rubber hose, closely studied her veins, then took out a syringe with an extremely small needle. Although Annie never looked when she had her own blood drawn, she fixed her eyes on Cassie's arm as though, by watching, she could make sure everything was done properly. She leaned her head so close to Cassie's arm that Jeff, as indicated by his white on blue name tag, gently asked her to move her head a little bit. As promised, he drew the blood and was done in very short order. The baby gave no sign of pain. In profound gratitude, Annie's eyes teared-up and she managed to eke out a small thank you. Jeff put a little Snoopy Band-Aid on Cassie and bid Annie good-bye.

The following day, Dr. Patterson called and told Annie that there were unusually high iron levels in Cassie's blood. She said her condition was quite rare and that she had, in fact, never seen iron levels so high in anyone – adult or child. She suggested they take Cassie to a blood specialist and gave them a referral in Kansas City. Three days later they were in Kansas City. The blood specialist did extensive testing – taking copious amounts of blood to do so. He came back with the same response as the pediatrician – the condition was extremely rare and he'd never seen such high iron levels. He had no idea what could have caused such a condition, then interrogated them on the possibility that Cassie could be, somehow, ingesting iron in the household either through feeding or something else with which she was coming into contact. Detergent? Blankets? Pacifiers? Bottles? Formula? Annie told Dr. Pinkerton that she was breast-feeding Cassie. Pinkerton then took blood from both Annie and Tyler to see if it was something genetic. It wasn't. Pinkerton was stumped and, noting that Cassie seemed, otherwise, to be in perfect health, he suggested they closely monitor the baby and watch for any signs of sickness – and weekly exams by the pediatrician for the coming month.

Both Tyler and Annie were beside themselves with worry. Annie got no sound sleep and was going to Cassie's room at frequent intervals throughout the night. On the night of August 10th, Annie found herself tossing and turning, unable to sleep. She went to Cassie's room and sat in the big rocking chair and watched Cassie in her crib. She prayed to God every few minutes to watch over her precious baby. She began to drift off when something caused her to awaken with a jolt. She looked around the room, frantically, in a confused state of mind. Suddenly, in the dim glow of Cassie's princess nightlight, she saw what looked like large figures standing in the doorway. She focused her eyes on this sight and wasn't sure what she was seeing. She cautiously rose from the rocker and took a step toward the door. She saw one of the figures make a slight movement. She screamed. The figure ran toward her and wrapped his arms around her ... putting a huge hand across her mouth. Two deafening explosions came from outside the room. She heard strange voices shouting from the hallway.

"Anjo's hit!!! He's hurt really bad!!! Oh God!!! I think he's dead!!!"

It was a female voice.

"Move Vinta!! Let me see!!"

A male voice.

"He's dead!! He's dead!! He shot him in the head!!"

"Where's the mother!!"

The female again.

"In here! I've got her!"

It was the huge man who was holding her.

Annie tried biting the man's hand but it was so tight against her mouth, she couldn't open it. The light in the room flashed on and Annie saw an enormous female coming toward her. She was smiling at her. She spoke in a soft, comforting voice.

"It's OK. You're safe. We won't hurt you."

Vinta could hear the woman trying to say something.

"Let her go, Tenu. She'll be all right."

Tenu Van looked at Vinta Zuly with a questioning expression but obeyed the order. He slowly took his hand from Annie's mouth. She immediately started shouting.

"Where's my husband?!!! What did you do to him?!!!"

Annie suddenly realized that the baby was crying very loudly. Tenu Van still had an arm around her. Annie spoke to the female in pleading tones.

"Let me get my baby!!"

Vinta nodded to Van and he removed his arm from around her body. Annie instantly ran to the crib and picked up Cassie, pressing her against her chest ... sobbing as she did. Vinta Zuly went to her and stooped to her level. She put a huge hand on the side of her face and spoke very softly to her.

"What's your name, sweetheart?"

Annie gulped down her sobs and eked out an answer.

"Annie."

"My name is Vinta. What's your baby's name?"

"Cassandra."

"Oh, that's a beautiful name, Annie. How old?"

"Almost two months."

"Is Cassandra a boy?"

"No ... she's a girl. I want to see Tyler."

"OK. But listen ... he's unconscious right now ... but he'll be fine. Do you understand?"

Annie nodded. Vinta put her left arm around Annie and led her out of the room. They passed a huge man standing outside the doorway with a rifle in his hand and another huge man, lying on the carpet. The side of his head was missing and the carpet under the remaining part of his head was soaked with a dark yellow liquid. Another male member of this assembly was kneeling beside the dead man. He stared at Annie as she and Vinta passed by. Tyler was lying on his back just inside their bedroom. His shotgun was across his chest with his right hand gripping it. Annie suddenly noticed the powerful scent of gunpowder in the air. She knelt beside Tyler and pushed the hair from his forehead with her left hand. She looked up at Vinta.

"Are you sure he's OK?"

"He's fine. He shot my friend, here, and we had to stun him with our rifles. He'll wake up shortly, I promise."

Vinta then asked Annie to move a little bit so she could put Tyler in his bed. Annie did and Vinta picked up the tiny man and effortlessly placed him on the bed ... covering him after she did. She looked at Annie.

"Why don't you and the baby sit on the bed with Tyler?"

Annie got up and did as Vinta suggested. Vinta smiled at her then went to Thanner, kneeling beside him. She turned off her voice convertor and spoke to him in Amburan. He did the same. He spoke to Benur and Tenu, standing outside the baby's room.

"Turn off your convertors."

Vinta looked into Thanner's face and saw his anger. He spoke to her with a tone to match his expression.

"That fucker!!"

"I know, Thanner ... I know. Poor Anjo ... such a kind soul. But this man was just protecting his family. You and I would have done the same thing. We were in his house to take his baby."

"I know that! Goddamn it!! But I've known Anjo for over a hundred years. We've been on so many missions together. He and Ben and I were like brothers. What a fucking mission ... taking babies out of their houses in the dark of night! What kind of people are we?"

Vinta stroked the back of Thanner's head. He knew she had fallen in love with him ... and he was fighting the same urge. It was entirely unprofessional for an officer of the Space Service to show such affection to another officer ... particularly in front of their crew – but at that moment he really didn't care. He felt tears coming to his eyes and touched them with a knuckle of his right hand. This brought tears to Vinta but she let them flow down her cheeks. It was soothing to her. Thanner took on a serious tone.

"What are we going to do with the female?"

"We've got to finish the mission ... so how about you take the baby and I'll stay with her until you get back."

"What about the male? He'll be waking up shortly."

"I'll anesthetize him. I don't want to deal with both of them ... and he's likely to have more weapons around, somewhere."

"OK ... that sounds good."

Thanner stood up and walked to the two remaining combat soldiers and explained what they were going to do. He came back and kneeled beside Vinta.

"How are you going to get the baby from her?"

"I'll handle it."

Vinta stood up, turned on her voice converter, went to the bed, and sat beside Annie and the baby. She put a hand on each side of Annie's face and brought her face close to Annie's. She talked in a voice just above a whisper.

"Listen, sweetheart ... I need to tell you something. We need to do a test on your baby."

Vinta could hear the frightened gasp coming from Annie.

"Don't worry Annie. Please trust me. I would never hurt your baby and none of these men would, either. What we're doing is necessary. I can't explain the whole story ... I just need you to trust me. Now listen ... I'm going to stay right here with you until they get back with your baby. It will be less than an hour, I promise. No one will hurt Cassandra. I promise you."

Vinta slid her hands from Annie's face and put her left hand on her leg.

"Will you trust me?"

Annie squeezed Cassie tightly.

"I'm not going to take your baby out of your arms. I want you to give me the baby on your own. This is something that has to be done, Annie."

Vinta brought both of her hands to her lap and sat in silence ... awaiting Annie's response. After several minutes, Annie held Cassie in front of Vinta and spoke to her as she did.

"I trust you, Vinta."

Vinta's heart jumped and she took a quick gasp of air. In that instant, she became the protector of Annie and her family. No one was going to do any harm to them. She would do what ever was necessary to make sure of this. Vinta took Cassie gently into her hands and brought her against her chest, placing her huge hand across the baby's back. Annie could tell she had nothing to fear. Vinta smiled at Annie then carried the baby to Thanner and gave her to him. Thanner held the baby in the rather stiff, awkward manner of a man. In Amburan, Thanner told Benur and Tenu to pick up Anjo's body and carry it to the ship. He followed them down the stairs.

CHAPTER 23

After her crew had departed, Vinta told Annie that she would have to anesthetize Tyler for safety sake ... assuring her, he would be fine and that the anesthesia would do him no harm, whatsoever. She then showed Annie the small wand and explained how she would use it on Tyler. Annie paused for a few moments then told Vinta to go ahead. Annie then invited Vinta to go downstairs to await her crew and Vinta accepted. They went into the kitchen and Annie was very embarrassed when she realized that all her chairs were much too small to accommodate Vinta. She blushed and was searching for words. Vinta put her at ease.

"No problem, Annie."

She sat on the well-worn, wooden floor and leaned her back against the pink-flowered wallpaper covering the kitchen wall. Annie asked her if she would like a cup of tea. Vinta thanked her but explained that the herbs and the water may contain elements that were intolerable to her system. With this, Annie forewent tea for herself and joined Vinta on the floor ... sitting a few feet to her right. They sat in silence for awhile ... both searching for a way that two females – from two different parts of the universe – could make casual conversation. Annie made the first try.

"Vinta ... umm ... where, exactly are you from?"

Vinta smiled at the broken silence and happily answered.

"Very, very far away. Over a thousand light years away. Do you understand light years?"

"Yes ... I do. That is really far. Does your planet have a name?"

"Yes ... it's called Ambura."

"What's it like?"

"Actually ... very much like yours. We call your planet GXM 731. What do you call it?"

"Earth."

"That's an interesting name. It's very short. What does it mean?"

"I don't think it means anything, really ... it's just its name. Is Ambura different than our Earth, in any way?"

"Oh yes ... it's not nearly as pretty as Earth – to begin with."

"Why?"

"You have a lot more colors than we do. Like your sky, for instance ... ours is constantly yellow ... but yours is a beautiful blue with pretty white water vapor."

"Those are clouds."

"Oh ... I see. And you have so many different types of weather and landscapes. On Ambura ... it's the same everywhere ... same temperature ... same kind of vegetation. And we don't have the frozen white water particles on the ground like you do in some places."

"Snow."

"Pardon me?"

"The white stuff ... it's snow."

"Oh ... I see ... yes."

"Vinta?"

"Yes?"

"You said this situation with testing Cassie was complicated ... can you please try to explain it to me?"

Vinta looked away and was in thought for some time. She finally looked at Annie.

"OK ... I'll try. First ... there are many beings from a number of space sectors here, on 731 – I mean Earth."

"Where?"

"Underwater. There are lots of sector bases in the really deep parts of your ocean."

"That's really funny. I told Tyler, one time, that I bet there were aliens living in those two really deep trenches we have in our oceans ... because we can't go that deep in the water and no one would ever know the aliens were there."

"Well, you were right, Annie ... and that's precisely the reason we put our bases there."

"I'll be darned. Wait 'til I tell Tyler. He always thinks I'm so crazy. But ... why are you people here?"

"Oh ... for the same reason you Earth people send out expeditions to your moon or down in your oceans or to remote parts of your planet ... because sentient creatures seem to want to know about everything. Your planet has been explored for millions of years, actually. First ... it was by beings from your own galaxy ... then, as space folding technology became widely spread, by people from all across the universe."

"What's space folding?"

"Well ... rather than regular travel ... like you do in your small transports on Earth – going from one place to another – in space folding we bend the distance between Ambura and Earth so it's right beside us – and we're here in an instant ... from a thousand light years away. Once we get here, the space folding is turned off and the space unbends. Very simple, really."

"Oh my gosh! ... I've seen that in Star Trek."

"What is star trek?"

"It's just a make-believe movie."

"Oh. Well, anyway ... Earth is on a no-contact list ... which means no sector is allowed to make direct contact with the natives."

"Why not? I've always hoped that space aliens would come down to Earth and help us with all of our problems."

"The results aren't good like that, Annie. The sectors have learned, by experience, that direct contact with primitive people by beings, much more advanced than they are, almost always wrecks their society. It just completely throws them out of kilter ... their view of themselves and their world ... and their religions. Their lives just don't make any sense to them anymore. It, almost always, deteriorates their cultures and throws their world into chaos. That's why in the Avantrees – that's the trans-sector governing body – they made it illegal for any sector to have direct contact with any natives on planets designated as primitive."

"This is getting really complicated."

"I know ... I'm sorry. But Earth is designated as a primitive planet and there have been two incidents of this

114

kind of illegal activity, here. One was about a hundred years ago. There was actually a war in the space around Earth over the intervention. I'm pretty sure no one on Earth knew anything about it. It ended when an Amburan warship blew a primary Enrue ship out of the sky ... and killed thousands of them – and they surrendered. It was on another part of the Earth – not near here."

"Was that the thing in Russia ... where hundreds of miles of trees were killed and no one could figure out how it happened?"

"I'm not sure where Russia is ... but, yes, it did wipe out many, many trees. It may be in Russia ... I don't really know. We were lucky it happened over a wilderness. But there's been another native intervention, recently, on Earth ... by the Olenreths."

"What did they do?"

"One of the worst things of all – they started a trans-genetic program."

"What's that?"

"They began extracting male and female natives ... and taking them to their medical ships and – using a mixture of the male and female and Olenreth genetic materials inside the female's egg – put it back into the female's womb. Then she would have a baby with a portion of Olenreth genes in it."

"Why would they do such a thing!!? That's horrible!!"

"Yes ... it is. That's why in the Avantrees, they made it not only illegal – but an act of war. And we are, at this moment, at war with the Olenreths for doing this."

"What do Olenreths look like?"

"Well ... this may sound elitist to you ... but I think they are ugly as sin. I've always said they look like reptiles."

Annie jumped to her feet, shaking. Both hands were in front of her mouth and her eyes were wide, in terror. Vinta understood, immediately. She stood up and embraced Annie. She then backed away and put a hand on each of Annie's shoulders and looked down, into her eyes and spoke softly.

"Some people remember these things, Annie. I'm so sorry it happened to you ... and that you have this awful memory. The Olenreths are, truly, horrible people. It's against my religion to say this, but I can't help it ... I really hate them. They are nothing but trouble and heartache for everyone. They don't care about anyone else in the universe but themselves. The members of the Avantrees just barely put up with them. They been expelled a number of times."

Annie started beating her hands on her thighs.

"Oh my God ... Oh my God ... Oh my God ... my baby ... my poor little baby ..."

Vinta pulled Annie up to a standing position and wrapped her hands around her, holding her tightly.

"It's OK, sweetheart ... It's OK ... everything will be OK ... I promise you."

This calmed Annie. Vinta felt her relaxing. Suddenly Annie pulled away from Vinta and stared at her.

"How!? How can things be OK!? They put their alien blood into my baby! How is that OK!? How? How?"

Vinta sat on the floor and asked Annie to sit beside her. Annie refused.

"Listen Annie ... I made a promise to you that Cassandra would be OK. I am going to do whatever I need to do to keep my promise. As I understand this trans-genetic thing ... they do it a little bit at a time. They plan to get Cassandra and you and Tyler, again – don't worry they never will, now – and take genetic material from her and mix it, again, with you and Tyler and their genes then put it back in another one of your eggs. You would then have another baby with an even greater concentration of Olenreth in it. On the fourth pregnancy, as I understand it ... you would have a baby that looks just like an Earth person ... but would be primarily Olenreth inside. It would be an Olenreth that could live on Earth."

"Why!!? Why would they do that!!?"

"Annie ... once they have enough of these Olenreth mutants on Earth, they'd take over. The Olenreths really like Earth – and they want it for themselves."

"Oh!!! Oh!!! Vinta!! It's awful!! It's so awful!!"

"It *is* awful, Annie. That's why were stopping them. They have no right to do this ... and no truly civilized people would do it!"

"But what about Cassie!?"

"All right ... here's my thoughts. First ... you need to understand the Avantrees' position on this. We're been ordered to surveil the Olenreths and locate every transgenetic subject on Earth. And then ..."

"What!?"

Vinta shook her head and went on.

"We're ordered to eliminate all mutant subjects."

"What!!!?

"Those are our orders, Annie ... but I'm not following them! I just can't! I'll be court marshaled, I know ... but I can't kill babies and I won't let anyone else kill them, either!"

"Well, what are you going to do Vinta?"

"I don't know, yet. I have to think about it. Think about what to do."

"But what *can* you do, Vinta? It's just you ... against everyone. I just don't know how you're going to do this."

"Right now ... I don't know, either ... but I'll see to it that no babies on Earth get killed. I promise you ... somehow, I'll do it."

Annie dropped to her knees, buried her hands and face in her legs and began weeping. Vinta slid across the floor to her and began rubbing her back.

CHAPTER 24

On the day following his death, as per Space Service tradition, the body of Anjo Manzy was taken by his crew into outer space and, following the prescribed military ceremony, with the crew in full military regalia, it was shot from the craft into space ... to float ... infinitely ... within the endless cosmos.

Following the ceremony, the crew gathered in a private room in the base's Officer's Club to remember and celebrate the life of their cherished friend. With the exception of Tenu Van and Vinta Zuly, those in attendance had all served for many years with Anjo on countless missions to exotic locations throughout the known universe. Tenu and Vinta respectfully listened to the plethora of tales told about Anjo and drank the copious toasts offered in his memory.

Vinta chastised herself for allowing the thought to enter her consciousness that Anjo's widow would now be given an Eligibility Certificate to have a baby. How could she think such a thing when Anjo's death was not yet a full day behind her? Anjo's head was blown off and she was experiencing envy of his widow. She was disgusted with herself. Was she really so overcome with female hormones that in the face of the tragic death of a comrade, she would feel envy over grief? This thought caused her to reflect on what she had pledged to do to protect the native babies. Was it morality – or just raging hormones? She had experienced a prideful moment for possessing the noble sentiment of saving the babies at the cost of losing her military career. Now, she was questioning her true motivation. The more she anguished over this, the more she drank. She had never in her life been intoxicated, but she knew this was going to be her first experience ... and she did not care.

In the early hours of the morning, Thanner Plegrue assisted her to her room, amid her nonsensical ramblings about incoherent topics. Despite the solemn occasion of the day, he found himself laughing at Vinta's antics. Inside her room, he lifted her into his arms and deposited her gently onto her bed. He was just beginning to stand up after pulling his arms from under her when she grabbed both his biceps in a vise grip and pulled him down to her face. She kissed his lips with quite a force. Drawing her face away from his, by only a few inches, she boldly proclaimed to him that she loved him. Vinta then dropped onto her pillow and, with a very happy smile on her face, passed instantly into slumber.

The next morning, the entire crew underwent cranial stimulation, via the crew's physician, who used an appropriate wand setting to eliminate the physical distress wrought by the previous night's activities. Medical Officer Erdevel used the wand on himself, as well. The initial stage of their mission was now complete, and the results of the tests were being put into a file for the assessment of Admiral Rite and his staff. The Enverton crew was given a three-day leave before the next phase of their overall mission. Nearly everyone elected to explore 731 in the small, two-person crafts available in the Base Recreation Center. Thanner and Vinta paired-off.

With no particular location in mind, they flew at an altitude of 10,000 feet ... perusing various parts of the fascinating sphere, flying with a deflection shield around the ship to avoid detection, either visual or by radar. They had brought a picnic lunch with them and looked for a nice place that was void of native habitation. In a tropical region, just south of the equator, they came upon an enormous island chain. Scanning each island for human presence, they finally located one that had none. They put their craft down on a beach of white sand and exited with happy excitement. The water was crystal clear, allowing them to see the ocean bottom, rich with brilliant hues. The island had mountains toward its center, covered with a tangled jungle of palm trees, tall grass, and a variety of small palm bushes. They could hear the lapping of the water and the strange sounds of birds hidden in the jungle.

The lovely fragrance of tropical flowers filled the air. The sun was warm and the ocean breeze was gentle. The dark blue sky had a few white wisps adorning it. Thanner had experienced this before on his previous trips to 731, but Vinta was overwhelmed with her first visions of this paradise. She stood, wide-eyed, spinning left and right, looking up and down. Finally, she looked at Thanner, speechless, with an open mouth. He smiled at her.

"It's something, isn't it?"

"Oh my God, Thanner ... no wonder the Olenreths want this for themselves. It's so beautiful ... it's beyond words. I really don't know how I could truly describe this ... this whole thing ... the colors, the soft, warm air, the beautiful fragrances ... the sounds. A person would have to be here to understand it. There's nothing you could do to allow them to truly appreciate it ... even pictures. You can't smell and feel and hear in a picture. It's so much more beautiful than Ambura, Thanner ... or any other planet I've ever visited. I wonder if the 731 natives truly appreciate what they have?"

"I doubt it. No one from this planet has ever seen another habitable planet, so they have nothing to compare it to."

"Do you know what Annie calls this planet?"

"No."

"Earth."

"Hmmm ... that's a rather odd name."

"I said the same thing. Ask me what the word Earth means."

"OK ... what's it mean?"

"Nothing."

Vinta laughed in a very girlish way.

"Annie told me that, too."

"Sounds like you and Annie did a lot of talking."

"We did. It's amazing ... there we were ... two people from galaxies a thousand light years apart ... and we were both comfortable with one another – as females. We had empathy ... and real affection for one another. I'll bet if you sat down with her husband and had a conversation with him ... you'd feel the same way. We all think we're so different from other sector species – especially primitive ones – but we're really very much alike ... same loves ... same fears ... same problems. Annie told me that she had always hoped that aliens from outer space would come down to Earth and solve all their problems for them. What she doesn't realize is that, regardless of how advanced civilizations become, they still have all the same problems they had when they weren't so advanced. I mean ... look at us ... we're dealing with the Olenreths – who are supposed to be so advanced, just like us. They're just a bunch of greedy jerks ... no different than the greedy jerks they were ten thousand years ago. They fly around in space, all over the universe ... and live forever – just like we do – but nothing about them has changed since they discovered fire. Same with us. Do you think Amburans have changed since Fenzen was discovered?"

"Oh, hell no. As a matter of fact ... I think we've, actually, lost a lot. I was just telling Remmy that, before we left on this mission."

"Who's Remmy?"

"My wife."

Vinta's expression changed and she looked down at the sand.

"Oh."

She was silent for a short while then looked up at Thanner.

"I'm sorry ... you've never mentioned her name before."

Vinta's expression could not hide her sadness.

Thanner looked around with quick head movements then flashed a bright smile.

"Let's have our picnic."

Vinta became embarrassed by her reaction to learning Remmy's name and it showed on her face. She forced a smile.

"Good idea."

They walked back to their craft and Thanner pulled out a blanket and their food basket. They walked to the line of trees about twenty yards from the surf. Vinta took the blanket from under Thanner's arm and spread it on the sand in the shade of a large palm tree. They sat down, facing the shore with the food basket between them. Vinta took out two plates and two fancy glasses, then laid a folded napkin on each plate. She then pulled out a bottle of Amburan wine and handed it to Thanner ... who opened it and poured a half glass into each. Vinta then began pulling out a number of closed containers from the basket, removing the lid from each before she arranged them on the blanket. They lifted their glasses and toasted one another, then took a small sip of the dark blue beverage. Thanner was hungry and immediately dug into the picnic food, moving from one container to the next, rather quickly. Vinta watched him as she did ... feeling an odd sense of possessing Thanner because he was eating the food she had prepared. Her heart swelled and a jumble of emotions percolated through her. Finally, Thanner noticed he was the only one eating.

"Aren't you hungry?"

"Oh ... I'm just watching you eat."

"You're going to make me self-conscious."

"Oh, I'm sorry, Thanner."

"I'm just kidding you. Look all you want ... I'm hungry."

He went back to eating with great ease. Vinta took a few of the nuts and some pieces of fruit and put them on her plate then nibbled at her collection. She was too excited to eat. For the first time in her life, she was in love. After a while, Thanner became satiated and leaned back on his elbows and straightened his legs in front of him. They watched the small waves lap the white sand. He realized he was happier than he had been in well over a hundred years ... not only with the beautiful setting ... but because he was with Vinta. His glow was somewhat diminished by his guilt but was still magnificently bright. Vinta moved the basket from between them and closed the gap between them. She took the pointer finger of her left hand and gently ran it up and down Thanner's cheek, then slid all of her fingers into the side of his hair and ran them to the back of his head. She then returned her left hand to join her right and folded them in her lap. Thanner rolled his face toward her then sat up, only a few inches from her body. He spoke to her in a quiet voice.

"Where's this going, Vinta?"

"I have no idea. You know I'm in love with you, Thanner."

"Yes ... I know."

"Well ... love goes where it goes. We'll both find out, won't we?"

Thanner smiled at her with obvious affection.

"I guess we will."

Thanner knew he loved her. He had no idea where it would lead. All he knew was that he felt like a very young man ... as confused and blindly happy as only a very young man can be.

CHAPTER 25

Admiral Rite called Captain Plegrue and Lieutenant Zuly to his office in regard to the test files on the dozen native infants their crew had extracted. All were confirmed to have been infused with Olenreth genes. With this information, he authorized the next stage of the mission – the boarding of all Olenreth vessels and the impoundment of their underwater base.

The impoundment and boardings would have to be done, simultaneously, to prevent a coordinated Olenreth resistance. This would require many more combat troops than just that of the Enverton. A courier was sent to the Dangean Sector Command Center on Hidresa with the information and the troop request. Ten days later, the troops began to arrive. Ten warships were Amburan and four were from other planets within the Dangean Sector. There were also some three hundred single-pilot fighters accompanying the flotilla. Among the Amburan ships, was a huge prison vessel – needed to house the thousands of Olenreth prisoners to be taken. Twenty more members of the elite Advid Squad were attached to the Enverton crew for this mission and were housed in the same barracks with them. The non-Amburan troops stayed aboard their ships since the base had an atmosphere incompatible with their physiology. All together, there were more than eight thousand troops in the attack force. Captain Plegrue was appointed commander of this large contingent. He selected Benur Iler as his second-in-command, feeling Lieutenant Zuly was simply too green to handle such an assignment. She offered no objections.

Plegrue divided the large force into five squadrons and appointed leaders for each. He would lead the squadron tasked to take the Olenreth Base. This was, by far, the most dangerous assignment, with an almost certainty for loss of life. Plegrue, as always, assigned himself to the foremost position of the attack force – continuing his commitment to "lead from the front." Benur Iler would also join him at the front. Lieutenant Zuly, who now viewed Thanner Plegrue as "hers," was beside herself with fear for his safety. Thanner had accepted his status as "hers" and had, in exchange, made an open commitment of his love to her, knowing not where this would lead. Such is love.

Working with Iler and the four other squadron leaders, Plegrue developed the battle plan. With surveillance, they were able to identify all of the Olenreth ships. Plegrue made assignments, giving specific responsibility for monitoring each Olenreth ship since, at the designated moment of the simultaneous boardings, the assigned units would have to know the location of each ship.

The evening before the coordinated attack, each soldier sought out whatever it was that might bring equanimity. Thanner and Vinta sought one another. They walked the parks in the Amburan Base, keeping to themselves. Eventually, they sat on a bench facing the large artificial lake. For a long while, they looked at the water in silence ... their love having made them comfortable with such a silence. Their mutual presence was sufficient communication. Vinta struggled with her fears of the morrow which eventually made itself known.

"Thanner ... you're the commander of the entire force tomorrow ... why do you have to be out front? Most commander stay behind ... why can't you? You're too valuable to lose."

"My mentor was my first commanding officer ... Captain Oplu. I served under him for almost fifteen years. He was always out front on every mission and I said the same thing to him about being too valuable to lose. He said to me ... 'Which would cause you to show more courage in battle ... following my orders or following my lead?' He didn't have to say anymore. I understood. It's one thing to order soldiers – it's another to inspire them. That makes all the difference in battle. There will be lots of seasoned veterans in the ranks tomorrow ... but every one of them will be frightened, going into battle. Most people don't understand that. They think we're fearless. Nothing could be further from the truth. But a good soldier can be inspired to bravery and nothing is more inspiring than to see your leader in front of you. And if you fall, your troops will be even more inspired to honor your death ... and do things they never thought they were capable of doing."

Vinta rubbed Thanner's thigh and looked into his eyes.

"I love you, Thanner Plegrue."

He covered her hand with his.

"I love you, Vinta Zuly."

"Thanner ... what are we going to do?"

"Stay together."

"But you're married."

"Remmy is very happy with her endless and risk-free life. I can't tolerate it. We've already come to an end ... all that's left is an official proclamation. You live by your emotions and your heart and so do I. Remmy thinks that sort of thing is silly. I think it's the only thing that gives any meaning to life. I would give anything to return to the days before Fenzen. Fenzen came ... and took away almost everything that made life beautiful."

"Then let's live in a no-Fenzen world."

"What do you mean?"

"Let's stay here. We can live, love, and die here. I'm not afraid of death. Our heavenly parents will welcome us home."

"Are you suggesting that we become deserters from the Space Service?"

"I hadn't thought of it that way ... but ... if that's what it takes then – yes – I'd do it."

Thanner was speechless and, open-mouthed, he stared at Vinta.

"You can't really mean that, Vinta."

"Yes I can ... and I do. And there's more ... I might as well tell you."

"What?"

"I made a promise to Annie."

'What are you talking about? What kind of promise?"

"I promised her that no babies from 731 would be killed."

"You can't make that kind of promise ... you know our mission."

"I made the promise ... and I'm going to keep it. We have absolutely no right to take the lives of these innocent babies."

"But they're mutants."

"They are still innocent babies. Think of Annie's baby. Her name is Cassandra. Annie loves that baby girl, every bit as much as any Amburan mother ever loved her baby. And Cassandra is only in the first stage of genetic transfer ... with only a small portion of Olenreth genes."

"How about the advanced mutants?"

"We don't know if there are any, yet. Each of these native gestations is nine months ... and, from what they told us, the complete process takes four gestations. That's almost four years. Do you think they've been at this for that long?"

"I really don't know. We won't know that until we seize all of the Olenreth records – and find out.'

"There's something else. I talked Doctor Erdevel about this."

"Are you crazy!!? He could bring you up on charges!!"

"Oh, Thanner ... do you really think I'm that stupid? It was just casual conversation ... and I simply asked him if Olenreth genes could be bred out of a population by the natives if they caught it early ... you know ... with the first gestation."

"And what did he say?"

"He said it could be done by selective breeding."

"Which means what?"

"That each person with Olenreth genes would have to have a baby with someone who had no Olenreth genes ... then that baby – when he grows up – would have to do the same thing ... have a baby with someone who had no Olenreth genes. He said it could take five generations or more ... but it could be done. So ... the gist of the story is that it really isn't necessary to kill these babies. The Earth natives can solve the problem, themselves, without anyone getting killed."

Thanner rubbed his mouth with the palm of his right hand then breathed, audibly. He shook his head back and forth then spoke.

"Damn it, Vinta ... "

"What?"

"I can see where this is going. You're right ... it's wrong to kill these babies. And if Erdevel is right ... it may not be necessary – at least with some of them. Now you've put me right in the middle. I'm an officer in the Space Service and I've sworn to obey the orders of my superior officers. You've decided to disobey direct orders and desert the Space Service ... which would make you a criminal ... and given that this is during the time of a declared war ... you could be executed for doing what you say you're going to do. As an officer – and now knowing what you're planning – I have an obligation to arrest you – but I love you more than life itself. I would live and die with you and give up my endless life for you ..."

He leaned forward and rested his forehead on the palms of both hands. Vinta allowed him his time for pondering then put her hand on his back and began rubbing it. She leaned downward to bring her mouth close to his ear.

"I'm sorry, my love. I'm sorry I've put you in this situation."

Thanner sat up but looked at the lake ... and not at Vinta. She continued talking.

"You asked me where this love is going and I told you it will go where it goes. Well ... this is where it went. You'll have to decide if you're going to let it lead us further ... or if you're going quit ... and walk away from it. It's something you'll have to do all by yourself. I can't tell you what to do. If you walk away, you'll have to do your duty as a Space Service Officer – and arrest me. If you stay with me and our love ... you'll put yourself in the same boat I'm going to be in. Either way ... I'll still love you. You can quit on our love, but nothing can make me stop loving you ... not even if I end up sitting in a military jail ... or executed."

Thanner turned to her. It appeared he was about to say something very important. Then he didn't.

"Let's walk some more."

Vinta nodded and they did.

CHAPTER 26

One hour before dawn, the Dangean Sector Force was in position for the simultaneous assault. Each Olenreth ship was on the screen of its assigned striker and the base assault squadron was waiting outside the Olenreth dome, just within the edge of the ocean darkness. Nerves were stretched and troops, dressed in full battle gear, repeatedly checked their weapons and mentally reviewed their assignments. Vinta Zuly sat alone on the same lake side bench she had shared with Thanner the evening before. Her arms were raised in prayer.

At the first light of dawn, Captain Plegrue transmitted the "go" signal and all squadrons moved in on their targets. Plegrue's squadron converged on all of the Olenreth's forty base portals, simultaneously. As expected, as they closed in on the portals – being unauthorized vessels – each portal emitted a piercing alarm and the gates quickly descended to close-off the entries. Prepared for this, the lead ship at each portal was a Rammer, specially designed to breach security gates. The Rammers sent several small missiles to destabilize the gates, then engaged their enormous blast engines to rapidly propel the thickly-plated ships through the damaged gates. The attack ships followed immediately behind the Rammer, and within a few minutes, each port was swarming with Dangean ships. Before disembarkation, the lead warships fired small missiles to take out the sealed doors that closed off the entrance into the main base from the port area. This was followed with a number of blasts from their stun cannons into the inner base area. The concussive blasts instantly disabled many of the nearby Olenreths.

A rapid disembarkation followed, with the troops running at full gallop down the ramps, along the port walkways, and into the base. As soon as they entered the base, they encountered a barrage of deadly neutron beams striking all around them. They took what cover they could find and returned fire with war-grade weapons – far more powerful than the standard weaponry kept on the Olenreth base. The large Dangean weapons blasted away the cover behind which the Olenreths were hiding, leaving them helplessly vulnerable. The troops fired upon the open targets, with their guns on kill mode, and Olenreths began dropping in large numbers. As was the nature of the Olenreth, however, there was no sign of surrender from any of them and guns continued firing from all quarters. Spotting a housing unit from which there was coming an enormous amount of gunfire, a Dangean, carrying a portable blast cannon, opened fire on the structure. The outer walls instantly crumbled, exposing a tightly packed crowd of Olenreths on every floor – many soldiers with weapons and quite a few women and children among them. The Dangeans continued firing, dropping the soldiers and, sometimes, women and children as well.

The battle went on for more than an hour, as the Dangeans claimed more and more territory – forcing the Olenreths into smaller and smaller spaces. The neutron blasts, coming from the Olenreths, greatly diminished as the battle progressed, both from the casualties and from their weapons having exhausted their power packs. Even without weapons, however, the Olenreths were still dangerous. They leapt from hidden spaces onto Dangeans, using anything they could find as a weapon, drawing the fighters into hand-to-hand combat. Finally, the sound of neutron firings came to an end, and the Dangeans began sweeping the base for any possible areas in which an Olenreth could be hiding. Determining the battle to have ended, Captain Plegrue ordered an immediate search for all injured or dead Dangeans. The final count was twenty-one dead, fifty-seven injured. The Amburan injured were rushed to the medical facility at their nearby base, and the non-Amburans were taken to their corresponding hospital ships in the space above 731. Captain Plegrue's right shoulder was deeply lacerated, slashed by a neutron beam, but he forewent care until all other injured troops were assisted. His friend, Benur Iler, finally persuaded him to be taken to the base medical facility ... pointing out the steady flow of blood from his wound. He departed in a small medical carrier and left Benur in command of the clean-up operation, including the seizure of all records.

The base medical center was very busy with all the injuries and medical personnel rushing from patient to patient, determining the relative needs of the injured. An emergency technician quickly sealed Thanner Plegrue's wound with a laser and shot serum into his blood system to both heal the injured tissues and to protect from any alien bacteria, with which he may have been infected during the battle.

Vinta Zuly saw the many medical transports speeding toward to the medical facility and she ran at full speed to the building ... wildly searching for any sign of Thanner. Each time a transport would pull up to the Center, she would rush to see who was carried out. They finally stopped coming and she felt herself coming down from her hyper state, allowing herself to inwardly smile as she silently issued a prayer of thanks. She had begun walking toward the port to which the returning troops would eventually arrive when another medial transport came into sight, rushing with great speed to the medical building. She swung around and sprinted after the vehicle. When she got to the facility, she saw two medical troops pushing a floating gurney through the doors. She caught up to them just as they were about to push the gurney into the emergency suite. When she saw Thanner's face, she felt her legs giving out and she put her hand on the wall for balance. She managed to get out Thanner's name. He raised his head and smiled at her then gave her an "all-is-well" signal as they disappeared into the suite. Her back slid down the wall and she came to rest on the floor. A moment later, she burst into tears.

CHAPTER 27

On the morning following the Dangean assault on the Olenreths, Thanner Plegrue was given the final casualty report. Fifty-one killed – eighty-seven injured. No one in his Enverton crew was killed, but the loss of life hit Thanner very hard. This was the largest assault force he had ever commanded ... and, by far, the most men ever killed under his command. Like most military commanders, he asked himself, time and again, if there were something he could have done to reduce the death rate – a different strategy, perhaps. Vinta tried to convince him that he had done his very best, but Thanner felt personally responsible for the death of every one of his soldiers. He now had the solemn duty of writing to the family of each deceased soldier. Just the thought of it brought tears to his eyes. And it was something he could not delay ... something he would not delay ... and he began hand-writing the letters within an hour of receiving the report. He would not dishonor the fallen warriors with a standard notification letter and, thus, spent many hours trying to express his sympathy and his laudatory compliments in ways that were unique to each of the fallen. For each soldier, he made a point of contacting a close buddy of the slain warrior to learn something of his heart and soul to blend into his letter. He worked until midnight the first day, then resumed early the next day. In all, it took him three full days to complete his task. As soon as he finished, he bundled the letters and sent them, via courier, to be delivered directly into the hands of the families.

The large assault force remained on and above 731 in the event the Olenreths had been able to send out a courier during the attack, to alert their sector. If they had, there was the distinct possibility that the Olenreths would send a battle fleet to 731. Admiral Rite had prepared for this possibility, and Dangean reinforcements were already steadily arriving. A growing spherical blockade was being set up, entirely surrounding the space around 731. Ships with the biggest weapons possessed by the Dangean Sector stood ready for battle.

It took base intelligence nearly two weeks to collect, organize, decipher, and analyze all the records seized during the Olenreth raids. From Thanner's point of view, the news was not as bad as he expected. Apparently, the trans-genetic program of the Olenreths was of fairly recent origins. To date, there were only one hundred live mutant births with thirty still in gestation. Thanner guessed the Olenreths had decided to start the program very slowly. All were in the first wave of the trans-genetic process. While this was good news, it complicated the issue with Vinta in that her argument that there was no need to kill the subject infants was reinforced. He considered, for a moment, the possibility of pressing this argument with Admiral Rite, but quickly dismissed it, realizing that not only was this a decision issued on at a Sector level but would appear that he was openly questioning his orders. Either way, he knew he had to reveal the report findings to Vinta, not only because she was his First-Mate but because he loved her.

As they were eating dinner at a base restaurant, on the evening of the day he received the reports, Thanner revealed the details to Vinta.. Before she had a chance to say so, he told her that it strengthened her argument.

"Why don't you make the point to Admiral Rite, Thanner?"

"I thought of doing it."

"Well ... are you going to?"

"No ... I can't."

"Well ... why not?"

"First of all ... I would be directly questioning my orders."

"So?"

"Vinta, please ... you're an officer ... you know the rules. Questioning an order is a court-marshal offense."

"But this is about killing babies."

"Vinta ... my love ... you're in the wrong business."

"Yes ... I've come to realize that."

They fell into in silence for a while ... each in thought. Vinta recovered first.

"What are you going to do, Thanner?"

"About what?"

"You know what I'm talking about."

"Talking to Admiral Rite?"

"No."

"What then?"

"Oh. Come on, Thanner. Are you going to arrest me?"

"No."

"Then what are you going to do?"

Thanner looked down then played with his food. Vinta waited. He pushed his plate away from him and then leaned on the table toward her with crossed arms. His face had a look Vinta had never seen before – a mixture of pain and determination. It made her afraid. She could feel her heart beating.

"I'm going to become a criminal with you."

Vinta pulled back, involuntarily, and stared at him. Her lower lip began to quiver.

"I hardly know what to say. I ..."

Thanner rescued her.

"You don't need to say anything, Vinta.. It's my decision. You don't have to feel as though you've led me into a life of crime. You're the one with the courage ... I had to convince myself to not be a coward. I'm the one who stands in admiration of you."

"But you're giving up so much ... everything."

"I'm giving up nothing. I'm in the Space Service because I can't stand my life on Ambura. I willingly put myself in danger to have some feelings about being alive ... to have some sense of purpose. You've given me a chance to do something for a truly noble cause – for love ... and to help you do something wonderful. I've never had a truly noble cause in my life. We may get caught doing it ... and be executed ... but it's something worth dying for. I'm about to become a deserter, and I've never felt better about my life than I do at this very moment."

"I've read all those old novels ... just like you,
Thanner ... but I never thought I'd ever be like one of the
characters. But here I am ... I'm in love with a man who is
willing to give up everything for me ... his reputation ... his
honor ... everything. And a man who will risk his life to
save innocent babies. We *are* a novel, my dearest."

Thanner chuckled.

"We'll write it, ourselves ... tell our story. Problem is ...
it just might be a really short story."

Vinta laughed.

"I don't care, Thanner. Whether we have a few months
together or a lifetime ... my life will have been worthwhile."

"So will mine, my dearest."

CHAPTER 28

A month after the Olenreth raids, the battle with the Olenreth Sector had not come to fruition. There had been a few scout ships sighted but, apparently, the Olenreths had decided not to engage in a Sector War. Resolving that the conflict had been averted, Admiral Rite sent orders to Captain Plegrue to begin making preparations for the final stage of their mission – the elimination of the mutant infants. They were to destroy the live births ... await the birth of the remaining gestations – then finish their work.

As soon as he got the orders, Thanner located Vinta and the two of them went directly to their, now traditional, lakeside bench. When Thanner told Vinta of his orders, she took an involuntary gasp of air and put both hands over her heart.

"Oh, Thanner. I knew this day would come ... but ..."

"I know ... it's still a shock. That's how I reacted when I got the orders."

Thanner turned to his left on the bench and looked Vinta directly in the face.

"I need to know, Vinta ... are you up to doing this? Once it starts ... there's no turning back."

Vinta paused noticeably, then answered.

"I'm scared, Thanner ... but I'm ready."

"Being scared doesn't bother me ... I'm scared, too."

"What do we do?"

"I've been thinking about it, quite a bit. We know the locations of all the babies ... and the females in gestation. We can't just take the live infants ... we'll have bring the parents, as well. We'll also have to bring the siblings along ... can't leave them as orphans. And with the pregnant females, we have to bring the rest of the family."

"That's a lot of people, Thanner."

"No kidding. Anyway ... Rite wants this last segment of the mission commenced with ten days ... so we've got to get moving right away. We need to decide where we're taking all these people. It's got to be somewhere remote ... without any present habitation, obviously. And with an environment that can sustain nearly four hundred people ... water ... food ... shelter. One of those remote islands won't do it. I think we'll have to look at the jungle areas. There are some very remote sections in those areas ... and the climate would be good for raising food and getting water."

"What are *we* going to eat, Thanner?"

"That's something else I've been thinking about. Kind of important, huh?"

Vinta smiled.

"It's going to be tricky. We'll steal as much food as we can manage ... but that will run out. I know, from talking to some of the botanical crews, here on 731 ... that Amburan seeds will grow in 731 soil – pretty well, actually. And they've experimented with eating some of the food they grew in the soil. Had some digestion issues at first ... but found that our bodies adjusted after a while."

"How about the water? Can we drink their water?"

"We'd have to filter it. The medical people say that we could probably adjust to 731 water if we became acclimated a little bit at a time. That's their theory, anyway ... nobody has ever taken it that far."

"Will our air converters work long enough?"

"The power packs, they say, are good for a hundred years ... so we'd have a good bit of time to think about it."

Vinta looked down, suddenly ... quickly enough to gain Thanner's attention.

"What's the matter, Vinta?"

She would not look up at him. Thanner put a finger under her chin and gently coaxed her head upwards. Her eyes expressed profound sadness.

"What is, sweetheart? Tell me."

Vinta hesitated ... Thanner coaxed. She finally and weakly spoke.

"What if I have a baby?"

Thanner froze. He had simply not considered the possibility and didn't know what to say.

"It could happen, honey. These things happen, you know."

"I know ... but ..."

"I want to have a baby, Thanner."

Thanner shook his head in understanding but still was at a loss as to what to say. A baby would present a whole new universe of complications. But it appeared that Vinta was quite resolute in her decision. He would have to deal with the practical challenges they would face with such a development.

"That's something I hadn't considered, Vinta."

"Well ... consider it."

"It ... I ..."

"OK ... let me. How can we arrange for our baby to breathe? Can we put a converter in him ... or her?"

"I don't know. It would have to be done right away ... and it would have to be pretty small. Also, we'd have to know how to do it. We're not surgeons."

"Well ... I'm going to find out."

"You'd better be careful."

"I will."

"Also, Vinta ... what would a baby eat?"

"Has it been that long?"

"What do you mean?"

"Women don't have breasts just for a male's pleasure, you know."

Thanner laughed.

"Oh ... yeah. I'm pretty dumb, huh?"

"No ... you're just a male. I'll forgive you for that."

"Well ... actually ... I've forgotten, but ... how long can you feed the baby?"

"A few years, if I have to. He'll eventually be eating whatever we're eating."

Now Thanner went into thought, which brought Vinta to inquiry.

"What are you thinking about, Thanner?"

He stared at her while he organized his thoughts.

"I'm wondering if it's right for us to have a baby."

"Why would you *say* that?"

"Well, Vinta ... just think ... who would he have, besides us? I mean ... who would he play with ... and when he grows up ... who would he have to ... well, you know ... girlfriends ... to marry ... that sort of thing?"

"Growing up, he'd have the Earth children. Kids are kids."

"But he'd be twice their size ... and he would be so much different than them ... the way we look."

"Well, we could have more than one baby, you know."

"Yeah ... I guess. It's just a lot to think about. But even if we have other kids ... he may never have a chance to do what we did ... get married ... have children."

Vinta thought for a few moments.

"Well, Thanner ... we going to have to steal a ship, anyway, to do this ... so steal a space-bender."

"Why?"

"Think about it, silly. When he's an adult ... we could take him to a planet where he could find an Amburan."

Thanner shook his head and gently chuckled.

"This is getting more complicated by the minute."

"Well, how did you think your life would be when you fell in love with a woman?"

They both laughed.

CHAPTER 29

During the following week, Thanner and Vinta worked in a near frenzy to plan their unlawful escapade ... hoping not to stir suspicion. Thanner carefully considered all of the various space vehicles available at the Amburan base. He finally decided upon the Lintoo – a very large, space-bending troop carrier used for large crew rotations. It had sleeping accommodations for over six hundred passengers with large eating facilities, recreation areas, medical facilities, and was equipped with very good weaponry. It also had several small, ancillary crafts onboard that they could use to extract the targeted subjects from the surface. Such a large craft would not only accommodate the transportation of his large group, but could also serve as temporary housing until the group was able to construct suitable outside housing.

Thanner and Vinta spent a good deal of their diminishing time flying a recreation craft in search of a good colony site on 731. They settled on an area in a subtropical jungle region that had both a large river and lake. They scanned the area for over one hundred miles in every direction and detected no human life forms. There was, however, an abundance of animal life throughout the jungle and also in the river and lake. After choosing the location, they decided on a good landing site for the huge troop carrier. They came back with neutron cutting tools and quickly cleared the landing area of plant and tree growth.

Next, they began stealing what they would need from the various base storage areas, including medical supplies, food, seeds, a portable generator, weapons, and a water purifier. Given Captain Plegrue's standing on the base, he had no trouble gaining entrance to such areas. Vinta looked for opportunities to engage Medical Officer Erdevel in friendly conversation – flirting when necessary – that led to discussing the medical information she needed.

As the week was nearing its end, they began working on the plans for actually stealing the Lintoo then on how to efficiently extract nearly four hundred natives from the surface. As for the extractions, it was fortunate that the Olenreths had used three cluster areas for the trans-genetic program with about forty infants and gestations in each. The dwellings were all in very rural areas, and the houses in each cluster were in close vicinity to one another. They could, therefore – using one of the large ancillary crafts, onboard the Lintoo – complete the extractions in a cluster area and then return to the home ship.

As for the actual extraction, they would have to move with great haste because they would have about two hours to do it. Thanner and Vinta would depart the base in the Lintoo as soon as night fell, and had to make the all the extractions and put the ship down on its landing site before the guard discovered it missing. As soon they did, the base would send out a fleet of scout ships to search for it.

The more they talked about it, the more troubled they became about their ability to extract so many people in such a short period of time. In fact, they would, likely, be able to rescue only a small portion of the families in two hours. Vinta came up with a possible solution. They could make a visit to Annie and Tyler and explain the situation, then ask for their help. A few days before their escapade, they could take Annie and Tyler onboard a small recreation craft and move quickly from one subject house to another. Annie and Tyler would go to the house and try to explain to the family what was going on and tell them to be at a selected site on the appointed night if they wished to be rescued. If the family had doubts about the veracity of their story, they could bring them to the craft. Thanner voiced his concern at such a blatant intervention and the possible ramifications if the subject families would communicate to the outside community about this. Vinta persuaded him that even if some of these families went public about their story, the chances of their being judged credible were very small. She pointed out how the intercepted communications on 731 demonstrated that such reports were treated with general disbelief and, often, ridicule. Thanner was persuaded, and that night, they set out for the McFarlands' home.

CHAPTER 30

On the morning following the encounter with the Amburans, Tyler McFarland awakened at a later hour than normal and found Annie at the kitchen table, drinking coffee and reading a magazine about babies. He sat across from her with a very troubled expression. Annie anticipated what he was about to say but simply smiled and bid him a "Good Morning."

He didn't reply and maintained his expression. He then stood up and got a cup of coffee, then sat down and took a few sips. He shook his head, slightly, back and forth, then after a pause, spoke.

"I had another nightmare, Annie ... but it was completely different this time."

He knitted his brow while trying to recall the details.

"This time ... I dreamed that a bunch of really big people ... with funny-looking hair ... were just outside our bedroom. I looked over to your side of the bed and you weren't there. I grabbed my shotgun, ran to the door and fired. I hit one of them in the back of the head and he went down. That was it. It was so real. Then I woke up and it was ten o'clock. Latest I've ever slept in my life. A very weird night."

Annie was about to reply then stopped to consider how to tell Tyler the real story. He wrinkled his face and responded.

"What?"

She put her right hand over her mouth and simply looked at him. Tyler raised his palms upward.

"What is up with you?"

"Oh my ... this is hard."

"What!? What is with all this weird bullshit this morning?"

"OK, Tyler. Sit back and take a deep breath."

"Jesus ... would you stop with the theatrics!?"

"Tyler ... it wasn't a dream."

"What the hell are you talking about?"

"It wasn't a dream, Tyler ... it really happened. I can show you the stain on the rug where the guy fell when you shot him."

Tyler was on his feet. He started walking back and forth, muttering "Jesus Christ" time after time. He wouldn't look at Annie. He appeared to be trying to get Annie's words out of his head. He finally walked to the kitchen sink and, with his hands on the cabinet edge, leaned toward the window, and stared at the field of corn in the distance. He was still muttering, under breath, as he rocked back and forth. Annie remained silent to let him deal with the shock of what she had just told him ... thinking about how she would have reacted had he told her something like this. After about five minutes, he returned to his chair and sat down. His eyes were closed and his head was tilted downward. Annie could see his chest heaving from his deep breaths. Finally, he raised his head, opened his eyes, and stared at her. The fear was undeniable. He had, intellectually, accepted that their previous encounter with space aliens had probably happened ... but it was an entirely different thing to have an alien invasion actually confirmed by your own wife ... willing to show you rug stains to prove it. He realized that there was an enormous gulf between conjecture and reality. The effect on his psyche was dizzying.

Tyler continued to stare at Annie and it became too unnerving to her. She had to do something or say something to end it. She spoke.

"Do you want me to tell you about it, honey?"

He didn't respond.

"OK ... I'll start and if you don't want to hear ... just say so ... OK?"

No response.

"All right ... here it is. The people in the hallway were from another galaxy ... from a planet called Ambura. They came to take Cassandra for medical tests to see if she had any genes from other aliens called Olenreths. There was a woman with them called Vinta who was really nice. She and I talked quite a bit together. She stayed with me until the rest of the crew got back with Cassie. They didn't hurt her, Tyler ... they were very nice to her. Now just try to stay calm about this next thing, OK?"

No response.

"Well ... OK ... you see ... these Olenreths ... who, by the way, are the frog face people we saw in out nightmares – but were actually here and actually took us away – have started this thing on Earth of making babies into Olenreths then taking over down here. These people from Ambura tested Cassandra to see if she's one of these babies, you see. Now she might not be, Tyler. Vinta told me, after they brought Cassie back, that they'd have to analyze her tests before they'd know for sure. She said she'd let me know."

Annie paused and studied Tyler. He was rubbing his forehead with his left hand. The hand was shaking.

"Are you OK, honey? Want me to stop?"

Tyler shook his head slightly in the negative.

"OK ... I'll go on. Now this is really the bad part. Vinta said that their orders are to come back and kill all the babies that have Olenreth genes – but wait!! Don't get all upset. She said she'd see to it that none of these babies are harmed. So don't worry. I trust her, Tyler ... I really do. You would too if you talked to her. She's such a good person ... or whatever you call her."

Tyler got up, took a glass from the cupboard, and filled it with water from the tap. He stood at the sink and drank half of it in several gulps then came back to the table and sat down. He cleared his throat several times then spoke. His voice was gravelly.

"Show me the spot on the rug."

He followed her up the stairs and she stopped about four feet down the hall from their bedroom. She pointed at the carpet in front of her feet. Tyler barely made out a large, yellow stain. He looked at her.

"This is it?"

"Yes."

"It looks like dog pee."

"I know. Apparently their blood is yellow. It was a real mess before I cleaned it up. I must have done a really good job since you haven't noticed until now. I saw the man laying here with all that stuff coming out of his head. You killed him, Ty. His name was Anjo ... and they were really upset about him dying."

"Well they shouldn't break into someone's house ... then he wouldn't be dead. What? Are you mad at me for killing him?"

"No, Tyler, no. You were just trying to protect us."

"Where were you?"

"In Cassie's room. I went in to check on her. Then these Ambura people walked in. I started yelling and that probably woke you up."

"I gotta tell ya, Annie ... I feel really weird right now ... calmly talking about space aliens being in our house ... like it's just a normal thing. But as I think about what you're saying, I'm starting to get really pissed."

"That's good, Tyler ... pissed is good. You were worrying me in the kitchen. I've never seen you so weird."

"What did you expect ... telling me I shot an alien from outer space in my hallway?"

"I know, Ty ... I know. I was trying to imagine if you had said that to me. I would have been a lot worse than you."

"Yeah ... you would. But the fact that these aliens are messing around with us like this really pisses me off. Who do they think they are? Do they think they can just play with us like we're toys? I'm sorry, Annie ... these big people who were here may be upset about their dead friend ... but tough shit! I'm glad I killed him. They had no right to just walk into our house uninvited."

"You're right, Tyler. They had no right."

"So ... when is this alien girlfriend of yours gonna to let us know if Cassie is OK?"

"I don't know. She didn't say when she'd tell me."

"Well ... I think our baby looks perfectly normal to me."

"Me too. Well ... she does have that weird blood thing."

"But she's perfectly healthy ... the doctor said so."

"Yep ... he did. Let's just keep our fingers crossed that she passes whatever test they did to her."

"That's another thing. Just the thought of those weird looking things taking our baby away with them. Goddamn it! It makes me want to shoot all of them."

"But Tyler ... Vinta wants to help us. She's going to protect Cassie."

"How do you know she is? How do you know you can trust any of these people?"

"I just know, Tyler. She's a woman and I'm a woman. I know when I can trust another woman."

"A woman from another galaxy."

"Yes ... but a woman."

CHAPTER 31

"Annie!"

Annie sat bolt upright in bed ... looking around her bedroom in her parent's old farmhouse.

"What is it, Bevvie?"

She got out of bed and walked to the door, looking for her older sister.

Tyler woke up.

"Annie ... where are you going?"

Annie turned and looked at Tyler. It wasn't her old bedroom.

"Annie!"

The female voice again. It wasn't Bevvie. Annie walked through the doorway and stood at the landing at the top of the stairs.

"Annie! Down here!"

Annie peered into the dark at the bottom of the stairs but couldn't make out who was calling her.

"Who is it?"

"Vinta."

Annie reached for the light switch on the wall to her right and flipped it upward. The ceiling lights came on in the upstairs hallway. She could see Vinta standing at the bottom of the steps.

"What is it, Vinta?"

Tyler appeared to Annie's left. He stared at Vinta.

"Can I talk to you?"

"Yes ... let me get my robe. She disappeared back into the bedroom. Tyler remained on the landing, still staring."

"Hi Tyler ... I'm Vinta."

He didn't respond.

Annie returned and started down the steps then turned back toward Tyler.

"C'mon Ty ... you come too."

Tyler nodded and went into the bedroom to get dressed in day clothes. Annie waited for him, then the couple descended the stairs together. Vinta embraced Annie as an old friend and then greeted Tyler again. He eked out a "Hi."

"I have my friend, Thanner, with me. He's on the porch. Is it OK if he comes in?"

Annie responded.

"Sure."

Vinta opened the door and told Thanner to come in. He stood beside Vinta and greeted the couple. Annie spoke.

"Well ... let's go into the kitchen ... OK?"

Vinta and Thanner nodded and followed them. Knowing neither of them would fit into a chair, Vinta proceeded to sit on the floor against the wall, and motioned Thanner to join her. Tyler turned his chair toward them and sat down. Annie followed suit. Tyler was struggling with the surreal moment and was studying the two giant aliens in his kitchen as one would an absurdity from a freak show. Annie noticed and called out his name in an admonishing tone, hoping the guests wouldn't hear. They did. Vinta intervened.

"It's OK, Annie. I'm sure we're quite a shock to Tyler." She smiled at Tyler.

"Don't worry ... we won't eat you."

This brought a slight smile to Tyler face and he relaxed a bit.

"I'm really sorry for staring ... but it's not too often I see space aliens in my kitchen."

Thanner and Vinta laughed.

Their sense of humor was immediately disarming. He liked them and kept talking.

"Can I ask you something?"

"Yes ... of course."

"How come you speak English so well?"

"What is English?"

"Ahhh ... the language you're speaking right now."

Vinta smiled.

"I'm not actually speaking English. I'm speaking Amburan ... but I have a device implanted in my throat that converts Amburan into English. And ... I have a thing in my ear that converts English to Amburan."

Tyler stared at her then spoke.

"Now that is something."

He looked at Annie.

"Can you believe that?"

"It's really crazy. Who would have thought, huh?"

Vinta got down to business.

"We need your help."

"What do you mean?"

"First ... about Cassandra. I'm sorry but she does have some Olenreth genes in her."

Annie gasped and covered her mouth. Vinta went on, quickly.

"But there's good news ... we found out that if you're careful, the Olenreth genes can be eliminated after a few generations. We'll tell you all about that later. Right now, we have an immediate problem ... and we need your to help us save all the babies that were affected by the Olenreths."

Annie spoke.

"Of course ... what can we do to help?"

Vinta looked to Thanner. He nodded and spoke.

"There are a hundred-thirty babies affected – some born – some still in gestation. We need to get both the babies and parents ... and maybe other siblings ... all in one night. That's a lot of people ... and we don't have time to go to each house to do it. The only way this will work would be to extract the people in groups at arranged sites. Here's where the two of you come in. We need you to go to each house that has an affected baby and meet with the family and tell them about the Olenreth problem and how we plan to save their babies. Then tell then where to be on the night we're coming for them."

Tyler responded.

"They'll think we're crazy."

"Yes ... we know. That's why we're going to transport the two of you to each house to explain this ... then when they think you're crazy ... you can bring them out to our craft to meet us. If that doesn't do it ... there's nothing more we can do for them."

Tyler thought about this for a few moments.

"Yep ... I think that should do it. If someone brought me to see a real flying saucer with huge aliens with funny hair standing in front of it ... that would do it for me – besides scaring the shit outta me."

Vinta stared at him then queried.

"What is a 'flying saucer,' Tyler? Apparently my converter can't translate that."

Tyler laughed.

"That's what we call alien spacecraft. Everyone thinks they look like a saucer – like a small plate that goes under a cup."

"Where did they get that idea?"

"In the movies."

Both Thanner and Vinta chuckled. Then Thanner continued.

"Now ... we need to do this really soon – beginning tomorrow. We don't usually do things in inhabited areas during the day ... but there are a lot of people to see and we'll need a lot of time to get it done."

"Won't people see us flying around?"

"No ... we'll use a light-bending screen around the craft. No one will be able to see it."

"Oh ... OK. I just thought of something. I have to work tomorrow, but ... wait ... what am I thinking? If you're coming to get us pretty soon ... what am I worried about Wal Mart for? Never mind. But ... when, exactly, is the night you'll be getting us?"

"Four nights from tonight."

"So ... that will be Wednesday night, right?"

"If that's what you call it ... yes."

Tyler stood up suddenly. He walked to the wall and took down a calendar hanging on a nail. He brought it to Thanner and sat beside him."

"I want to make sure we're both talking about the same night. Now this is today ... right here. We call it Saturday night ... but it's actually early Sunday morning. So show me what night you'll be coming ... OK?"

Thanner studied the calendar.

"OK ... let's both call this Saturday night, all right.?"

Tyler nodded.

"So ... this is the night we'll be coming."

Thanner pointed at the day.

"Is this Wednesday?"

"Yep ... that's Wednesday."

"OK ... then we'll be coming on Wednesday night."

Annie jumped in. She looked frightened.

"Where are you taking us?"

Vinta answered.

"To a very nice place, Annie. It's in a jungle area – far away from any other people. It's sunny and warm and has lots of trees and flowers ... and a beautiful lake and river. It will be a wonderful place to raise Cassandra. I'm sure you'll like it."

"Are we talking Earth, here, or some other planet?"

"No, no, no ... Earth. I should have said that."

Annie smiled, then a look of sadness came over her.

"I may never see my family again, Vinta."

"Yes ... I'm sorry but that's true. If I were you ... I'd tell them, soon, that you will be going away for a very long time but that you can't tell them why. So they won't worry when they can't find you."

Annie's eyes filled with tears as she looked at Tyler. He slid his chair next to hers and put his arm around her shoulders. She put her face on his chest and quietly cried. Thanner and Vinta respected her sadness and were silent. After a short while, Annie recovered, wiped her eyes and blew her nose. She forced a small smile.

"I'm OK, now. It's just hard, that's all."

Vinta's face showed her empathy and Annie appreciated it.

Thanner had a thought and offered it.

"Vinta and I are bringing seeds with us to grow Amburan food. I suggest you and the other families do the same. There will be some edible plants and fruit where we're going, I'm sure ... but not enough to sustain a large community for long. And the community will only grow larger."

Tyler responded.

"That's no problem. You're talking to a farm boy, here. I'll go over to the feed store tomorrow morning and get plenty. Then you watch the crop we grow ... Annie and me.

Vegetables, wheat, corn, fruit bushes, carrots, potatoes ... just you wait."

Vinta beamed.

"That will be wonderful, Tyler. It's great to have a farmer along."

"When will you be coming tomorrow?"

Thanner responded.

"We're keeping you up late tonight ... and you want to get your seed in the morning. When will you be up ... and how long will it take to get your seed?"

"I *would* like to get a little sleep tonight. I'm beat. How about we get up about nine ... have breakfast ... get cleaned up ... then I'll drive into town and get the seed. Should take about an hour. So how about if you come around noon?"

"What is 'noon'?"

Tyler took off his wristwatch and sat beside Thanner. He moved the hands to the twelve o'clock position and showed it to Thanner.

"This is noon. You take this watch with you and when it looks like this, then it will be noon. OK?"

"All right."

Tyler set the hands back to 2:37 and handed the watch to Thanner. He studied it as one would an artifact.

Cassie's cry reached them in the kitchen.

Annie got up.

"I need to get the baby."

Vinta responded.

"Are you going to feed her?"

"Yes."

"Would you mind if I watched you?"

"Of course not."

The women departed and the two men conversed.

CHAPTER 32

Tyler arrived home at 11:35 from his trip to the farm supply store. He left the many bags of seed, potted berry bushes, and small fruit trees in his truck bed and hurried into the house. He shouted for Annie. Her response came from the upstairs. He ran up the steps and found her in the nursery, dressing Cassie on the bassinet. Without turning, she spoke to him.

"Where in the world have you been?"

"Every farmer in South Nebraska was there today. I almost left, but then thought I might not get another chance to do this before we leave on our big adventure."

Annie picked up the baby and extended her toward Tyler.

"Here ... take the baby ... I'm not even dressed yet. No makeup ... my hair's a mess. I have no idea what to wear."

She glanced at Cassie's princess clock.

"Look at the time! They'll be here in fifteen minutes!"

She rushed past Tyler and ran down the hall to the bathroom. Tyler's experience with Annie under such circumstances dictated that he should make himself scarce. When he reached the bottom of the stairs, he suddenly jumped backward and nearly fell on the bottom riser. Standing just outside the screen door was Vinta. Her unannounced, gigantic form had startled him. Seeing his reaction, Vinta apologized.

"I'm sorry, Tyler. I'm not sure of the proper manner of announcing myself on Earth."

Tyler recovered his balance, equanimity, and lost dignity ... enough to respond.

"Oh ... that's OK."

He opened the door and stepped onto the porch. He smiled at Vinta.

"Sometimes people have a doorbell. It's a little button to the right of the door. If they have one of those, you just push it. It makes a sound inside the house and the people know you're at the door. We don't have a doorbell ... so you would knock."

Tyler demonstrated a knock.

Tyler heard Annie shouting from the bathroom.

"Tyler!! Answer the door!!"

He shouted through the screen door.

"That was me knocking!!"

"What!!?"

Tyler muttered to himself.

"Oh Christ."

Then shouted.

"Never mind!!"

He invited Vinta inside and told her to make herself comfortable. She didn't appear to understand the term, so he had her follow him into the kitchen. He extended his hand toward her traditional spot on the floor then asked if she'd like to hold Cassandra. Vinta said she'd love to. Tyler gave her the baby and walked upstairs. Annie was brushing her teeth in the bathroom. She spoke through the foam.

"Why were you knocking on the door?"

"I was showing Vinta how to announce herself."

Annie spit in the sink.

"What?"

"Vinta ... I was showing her how to knock on our door."

Annie stared at Tyler as though he were crazy then flashed an expression of comprehension.

"Vinta's here?"

"Yep ... she's down in the kitchen holding Cassie."

"What time is it?"

"About ten to."

"She's early."

"Yep."

"Is Thanner there, too?"

"Nope."

"Why not?"

"I have no idea. Maybe he's in the spaceship."

"Well go down and keep her company. Tell her I'll be down in a minute."

"OK."

Tyler sat in the kitchen with Vinta for ten uncomfortable minutes ... neither finding much to say to the other ...Vinta filling the time by adoring and cuddling Cassie. Annie came to his rescue at noon on the dot. She had on a yellow summer dress with a very well-stuffed baby bag on her shoulder which she immediately handed to Tyler. Feeling the weight, Tyler asked her if she was packing for a week's trip. She didn't laugh. The McFarland family followed Vinta to the recreation craft ... sitting in an opening within a cluster of trees about a hundred yards from the house. It was not shaped like a saucer. It was a boxy, black, triangular vehicle with no apparent windows. As they neared it, a ramp smoothly descended from the back end of the triangle. Onboard, they greeted Thanner who directed them to some comfortable seats. He closed the ramp and began moving his fingers on a flat screen lying on his lap. They could immediately feel the craft floating ... as though it were on water. Suddenly, the walls around them seemed to disappear, and they could see outside in every direction, as though they were sitting on their front porch. They were already very high above the ground without having had any sense of motion. The land below spread out before them at great distances in all directions. Visually, they could see they were moving at an extremely rapid rate but had no physical sensation of it. Annie began to feel dizzy and closed her eyes. Vinta sat beside her and spoke to her.

"Are you OK, Annie?"

"I never liked amusement park rides."

"I don't understand."

"Moving so fast makes me dizzy."

"Thanner thought you'd enjoy the transparent walls. Shall I have him turn it off?"

"No, no ... I'll get used to it."

Tyler piped in.

"Man ... I think this is great. Invisible walls! Who would have thought?"

In about ten minute's time, the movement stopped and they could see they were descending very rapidly. Annie thought she was about to get sick and squeezed Tyler's forearm in a near death-grip. In a few seconds, they were on the ground. They were on a large farm and could see a big white house in the distance. Thanner lowered the ramp and the McFarlands descended it. It took them about five minutes to walk to the farm house. Annie knocked on the screen door. A woman, wearing her Sunday clothes and an apron, came to the door and smiled at them through the screen.

"Hi there ... can I help you?"

Annie answered.

"Can we talk to you for a few minutes?"

The woman paused then opened the door and invited them in. Annie quickly introduced her family.

"I'm Annie McFarland and this is my husband Tyler, and our baby's name is Cassandra."

"She's beautiful. I'm Angie Reynolds."

"You have a baby boy, don't you?"

"Yes ... how did you know that?"

"That's why we're here, Angie."

"What do you mean?"

"Is there somewhere we could sit down?"

"Of course ... excuse me ... I should have asked. Let's go into the kitchen."

They followed Angie Reynolds and found her husband at the table. It was apparent they were about to eat. Annie was quite embarrassed."

"I am so sorry. I should have known you'd be eating right now ... right after church. How about Tyler and I go sit on the porch until you're done."

"Don't be silly ... sit down. Have you had lunch?"

Tyler jumped in.

"I haven't eaten since breakfast. I'm starved."

Annie looked at him with wide eyes.

"Tyler!"

"Well I am."

Angie laughed.

"Please ... sit. This is my husband, Earl."

Earl stood and shook hands with Tyler and nodded to Annie. Angie fetched two more plates from the cupboard and put them in front of Tyler and Annie. She motioned to the generous spread of food on the table.

"Help yourself."

Annie responded.

"Thank you so much. You've very kind."

Tyler immediately began loading his plate.

As soon as they had all filled their plates and settled into eating, Angie inquired.

"So ... are you two from around here?"

"We're from Finley."

"Where's that, exactly?"

"About a hundred miles west of Kansas City."

"You're pretty far from home."

Annie was flummoxed. She had no idea where they were and had no idea how to inform Angie and Earl of this weird circumstance.

"Listen ... I'm about to tell you some things ... and you're going to think I'm crazy ... but here goes. We have something in common with you. Both of our babies have the same problem."

Both Earl and Angie wrinkled their faces in bafflement.

"I hardly know how to tell you this. If you told me the same thing, I'd think you were nuts."

The couple wore frozen stares.

"OK ... here it is. We found out that our baby has genes from an alien race called the Olenreths ... and so does your baby."

Earl and Angie looked at one another then looked at the McFarlands with growing suspicion. Earl entered the conversation.

"What, exactly, are you two up to, here?"

Annie face burned with embarrassment. She was speechless at being suspected of foul play. Tyler spoke up.

"Look ... we knew you'd think we were crazy. But we're trying to save your baby."

Tyler stood up.

"Earl ... come look out your screen door for a minute, OK? I want to show you something."

Earl remained seated and perused the invitation then began to slowly get up with a look of skepticism on his face.

"Listen ... if you try anything, buddy ... I've got a shotgun in the next room."

Tyler smiled.

"Don't worry, Earl ... I'm not up to anything. Just look out your screen door."

The two of them walked to the front door. Tyler stood to Earl's left.

"Look over there ... about a hundred to the left of your gas well."

Earl looked.

"See that big black thing there?"

"Yeah ... what is that?"

"Now you're going to think I'm a madman ... but it's a spaceship."

Earl turned his face toward Tyler's and studied it. He pressed his lips tightly together then spoke.

"Well let's just go see."

Earl pushed open the screen door and motioned for Tyler to proceed in front of him. When they were both on the porch, Earl stopped suddenly and re-entered the house. He quickly came back out with a shotgun in his hand. They began the long walk toward the black object. The closer they got to the craft, the more puzzled Earl looked. When they arrived at the side of it, Earl was wide-eyed and open-mouthed. Tyler turned toward him.

"Earl ... you'd better put that gun down. The people inside this thing may not like it. They're very friendly ... but they'll protect themselves if they have to. You understand?"

Earl nodded and gently laid the gun on the grass. As soon as he did, the ramp descended, and a few seconds later, Thanner and Vinta emerged. Earl began backing up and looked as though he were about to start running. Tyler grabbed his arm and looked him in his eyes. Earl was shaking.

"Earl ... listen ... these people won't hurt you. They want to help us. There are other people who will be coming after my Cassandra and your little boy ... to kill them ...

because they have alien blood in them. These two are willing to rescue us. Do you understand me?"

Earl stared at Tyler and didn't respond.

"Earl! Run up to the house and tell the girls to get down here. Your wife needs to understand this ... and understand it quick. We have a lot of other people we need to warn about this ... so hurry up!"

Earl looked at him then broke into a sprint to the house. He ran into the house and thirty seconds later, he emerged with Angie and Annie, carrying Cassie. They hurried back to the space vehicle. Angie approached with her hand over her mouth and fear in her eyes. Tyler stepped up to her.

"Did Earl tell you what this is all about?"

"He was talking really fast ... but he says these people are here to rescue our baby."

"That's right. Now listen. We don't have a lot of time. There are a hundred thirty families that have a baby with alien blood and you're the first family we've talked to. We have a lot more stops to make. Now look ... if you want your baby rescued ... be at Clinton, Missouri on Wednesday night, as soon as it gets dark. There's a big field one mile west on route eighty-six. These people will be coming with a really big ship. We'll be with them. They're going to take all the families to a safe spot, here on Earth. They say it's beautiful ... a great place to live. We can't come back, though. They'll be looking for us. Now ... bring what you can carry in your truck. We need food for now ... and seeds and fruit bushes for the future. Get what you can ... and bring them on your truck to the landing spot."

He looked at Earl.

"You get all that?"

"Yeah ... I did."

"Will you be there?"

Earl and Angie looked at one another and both shook their heads in affirmation.

Tyler shouted to Thanner and Vinta to come over to them. As they walked toward the group, Annie and Tyler could see Angie and Earl stiffen. As the alien couple approached, both displayed wide smiles. They stopped a few feet from the new couple and looked down at them. Vinta spoke.

"Hi ... I'm Vinta Zuly and this is Thanner Plegrue. We're from a planet called Ambura. That's very, very far from Earth. We want to help you save your baby. I hope you'll let us."

Angie spoke in a shaky voice.

"Thank you very much. I'm scared ... but I believe you about our baby."

"What's your baby's name?"

"Tommy. He's named after Earl's brother. My name is Angie and this is my husband, Earl."

Both Thanner and Vinta extended their hands. After the handshakes, Thanner spoke.

"Do you clearly understand the plan ... where to be and when?"

Both answered in the affirmative.

"OK ... then we need to go. We have a lot of people to talk to. We will see you again on Wednesday night."

Thanner began walking back to the ship and motioned the rest of his party to follow. They quickly climbed the ramp and disappeared into the black triangle. The ramp closed and a few moments later, Angie and Earl saw the craft floating a few feet above the ground. In the next moment it was out of sight.

CHAPTER 33

The visits to the subject homes took much longer than anticipated. Thanner and Vinta had planned to end their home visitations before nightfall on the first day but the slow progress required them to continue until nearly eleven o'clock at night. Such was also the case for the following two days and the final visit was made at midnight on Tuesday. Not every family accepted the rescue plan. Some physically pushed Annie and Tyler out of their homes ... taking them for either insane or suspecting them of some nefarious plot. Out of the one hundred-thirty families with a gene-altered baby, only ninety-five committed to being at the location sites on the appointed night. Vinta was quite distraught that so many babies would be killed. Thanner was ambivalent. He was sorry for the families who would lose their child but relieved that the number of extractions was reduced to a more manageable number ... and that there would also be a reduced demand for the limited resources at the colony site.

Wednesday was surreal for Thanner and Vinta. They tried to go about their day as normal as possible, but the tension made it nearly impossible. They avoided the rest of the crew as often as they could to review details of the operation. The items they had systematically stolen from base storage areas were hidden nearby the docking space of the Lintoo. They had also commandeered several floating carriers to transfer their booty to the ship, which were also conveniently stowed. Each kept proffering the question ... "What have we forgotten?" As always – with any grand plan – the fear of an omission was what kept their tension level consistently elevated.

As the day was winding down and the artificial dusk approaching, neither Thanner nor Vinta could sit down. Their anxiety kept them on their feet and moving. At one point Thanner seemed sure that Ben Iler had looked at him, suspiciously. He mentioned it to Vinta, who brushed it aside as "anxiety generated paranoia." This somewhat placated Thanner, but he couldn't get Ben's expression out of his head. Finally, as the base lights dimmed to full darkness, Thanner and Vinta staged a chance meeting in the living area of their housing unit. Vinta appeared in the archway of the room and asked the seated and chatting Thanner if he'd like to take a walk. To knowing glances he tacitly acquiesced. The moment they got outside, Vinta tightly gripped Thanner's hand – not as a lover but as someone overwhelmed, who needed assurance.

He turned his head toward her and spoke quietly. "We'll be fine."

She gave her grip additional pressure as a response – but did not let go. They forced a slow stroll to their park bench and sat there for a short while – in the event any crew member happened to have walked out of the unit after them. Looking around, casually, and seeing no one from the crew, they got up and strolled to the downtown shop area, nodding to base acquaintances. Their path gradually arched toward the base docks. They slowly walked beside the small stream that led to the docks and bid a warm "Good Evening" to the guard at the entrance to the dock area. He responded with a salute and a reply greeting, using their names and ranks. As always, the dock area was entirely deserted. Thanner and Vinta had, over the past two weeks, made frequent strolls to the dock area to habituate the guards to their pattern of choosing to walk the lonely area at night ... allowing them to formulate a likely suspicion as to their motivation – which wasn't related to ship-stealing. They had begun to detect knowing smirks as their nightly soirées mounted in number. Seeing them, the pair smiled at one another in accomplishment.

After traversing the large area for a time, they eventually made their way to the dock harboring the Lintoo. They waited for the guard to make his rounds through the Lintoo dock. As soon as he departed the area, they knew the two-hour clock had started to run. Once inside the enclosed dock, their pace quickened to a near run. Thanner went immediately to the dock's alarm system and, using his officer's code, disarmed it ... allowing them to enter the Lintoo without setting it off. They hurried to the area where they had stored their supplies and began loading two of the huge floating carriers. Once they were loaded to capacity, they pressed the anti-gravity buttons and the floats rose about a foot above the ground. Pulling their weightless sleds, they climbed the ramp and guided them to an open area just inside the door. Pressing the buttons, again, the carriers gently descended to the floor of the ship. They hurried back to the storage area to load the two remaining carriers. Thanner loaded his faster than Vinta and he told her he was going ahead.

Just as Vinta was loading the last few items onto the carrier, she heard a man's voice shouting loudly. It wasn't Thanner. After a few moments, she realized it was Ben's voice. She walked to the wall – behind which they had stored their supplies – and carefully peered around the corner. Thanner was standing, halfway up the ramp. Ben was on the dock, at the bottom of the ramp. He had a beam gun pointed at Thanner.

"What are you doing, Thanner?"

Thanner was silent for a few moments then replied.

"Go back home, Ben."

"I can't let you take this ship, Than."

"I'm going to, Ben."

"Why? For God's sake, why?!"

"I can't let them kill all those babies, Ben."

"It's orders."

"Doesn't make any difference."

"Than ... we've done it before."

"I know we have ... and I've never gotten over it."

"You took the Oath."

"Yes ... I did ... but some things are bigger than the Oath."

"Not to me."

"Look, Ben ... please ... you're my best friend in life. Just let me go."

Benur paused.

"Can't do that, Than."

"Then you'll have to shoot me, Ben. And if you do ... put it on kill ... as a favor to me."

In a flash, Thanner saw Vinta rush Ben from behind. She slammed her shoulder into the middle of his back with remarkable force. It knocked him eight feet forward and he landed on the ramp, face-down. Thanner rushed toward him and stepped on his right forearm, pinning it to the ramp then pulled the pistol from his hand. He put the gun on stun and immediately shot Benur. Vinta looked at Thanner with wide eyes.

"The stun won't give us enough time, Thanner! He'll be conscious in an hour! He'll alert the base and they'll have the sky filled with search craft long before we're loaded and down!"

"What do you want me to do?"

"You have to kill him, Thanner!"

"I can't kill Ben! Are you crazy!?"

"Then give me the gun ... I'll kill him."

"No, Vinta!"

"Just stop and think, Thanner. If he wakes up and sounds the alarm ... we'll be captured – us and all the families ... then they kill the babies – and probably all the families. Then *we're* probably executed. Is that what you want? Either he dies or hundreds of Earth people die ... adults and children. Take your pick."

"I'll just tie him up ... and gag him."

"First ... we don't have the time for that ... we've barely enough time, right now, to make the extractions and get to the landing site before they come looking for us. And can you guarantee me that you're such an expert in tying people up that he won't get loose?"

Thanner dropped to his knees. Vinta saw the tears running down his cheeks. She stepped over Benur and went to him. He looked up at her.

"We've been in so many battles together. He's saved my life more than once ... and I've saved his. We know everything about each other. He's closer than a brother ..."

His head dropped and he stared at the ramp below him.

"Thanner."

He did not look up.

"Thanner!"

Slowly he raised his face.

"Give me Ben's gun and go inside the ship."

Thanner stated at her.

"Now, Thanner!"

Thanner put his hands on the ramp and pushed himself up. He handed the gun to Vinta then turned and slowly walked up the ramp and disappeared into the giant ship.

A few minutes later, Thanner saw Vinta enter the ship's main portal with her floating carrier in tow. She pushed it beside the others and pressed the anti-gravity button then shouted to Thanner.

"Let's go!!"

CHAPTER 34

Thanner piloted the Lintoo through the docking portal and into the open water then carefully traversed the ocean black to the surface. Although he had flown a number of space craft in the service, the Lintoo was, by far, the largest he had steered and was, thus, more cautious than he had ever before been. He broke the water's surface and, engaging the anti-gravity drive, he was at cruise altitude in seconds. He was about to enter the coordinates of the first rendezvous point when Vinta interrupted him. She was shouting.

"We've got move really fast, Thanner!"

He looked up at her. She was a study in panic.

"What?"

"Hurry!"

"I am."

"Thanner ... we have less than an hour."

"No ... we have nearly two."

"I couldn't kill him, Thanner."

"What?"

"Ben ... I couldn't kill him. He'll be conscious in less than an hour!"

"Good God, Vinta ... we'll never make it!"

"We have to!"

Thanner stared at her for a few seconds then rapidly spun in his chair to face the navigation screen. He reached into his pocket and pulled out his communication pad then copied the coordinates he had entered there, onto the screen. He pressed the course engagement icon and in an instant they were hovering over the first site. He took manual control and carefully lowered the Lintoo down to the ground. The slowness, that his inexperience with such a large craft induced, was nearly maddening. It was exacerbated by Vinta's shouting "Hurry!" on a number of

occasions. He nearly lost his temper with her but, knowing he had to remain focused on the task, he sublimated his rising passion by sheer will. He touched the ramp icon and it began lowering to the ground.
Thanner and Vinta sprinted to the exit area and ran down the ramp. There was a large crowd of people on the open field with wide eyes. Each family had a large assortment of possessions with them, laying all over the field. Thanner looked at Vinta and shook his head. He advanced to the edge of the crowd and shouted to the assembly.

"We've had some problems and we have only a very short period of time to pick up all of the families and get to our landing site. I'm sorry, but just take what you can carry and get on board as quickly as possible!!"

The people looked at one another then quickly did as they were told. Anyone big enough to carry anything grabbed something and the crowd shuffled toward the Lintoo and up the ramp. Thanner stayed on the ground, hustling the crowd up the ramp as best he could. Vinta stationed herself at the top of the ramp, guiding the awe-struck pilgrims to a large lounge area. By the time everyone had boarded and Thanner had resumed his seat at the controls, twenty minutes had elapsed since they had left the underwater Amburan base. In approximately thirty minutes, Benur Iler would regain consciousness, and soon thereafter, Amburan scout ships would be canvassing the planet for the missing Lintoo. Vinta Zuly glanced at her time device and a wave of near-panic swept over her. With the passengers settled onboard the Lintoo, she rapidly traversed the very long passageway from the lounge area to the pilot's station. By the time she got there, they were already at cruising altitude and Thanner was in the process of entering the next coordinates into the navigation screen. She quietly informed him of the quickly dwindling time ... to which he simply closed his eyes momentarily then proceeded with his task without responding.

In a heartbeat, they were hovering above the second point of rendezvous. Once again, Thanner went manual and he guided the Lintoo to a soft landing on an expansive, harvested wheat field. They completed the boarding process, and with about twelve minutes remaining on the allotted time clock, they set out for the final landing site where the McFarlands would be waiting with their assembled entourage. As the passengers were climbing the ramp at the fastest pace they could manage with possessions hanging from various parts of their bodies, Vinta saw the hour time limit pass. She felt an urge to scream but managed to keep her feeling of terror under control. Thanner engaged the antigravity drive the moment the screen indicated the ramp was closed. He knew the Amburan search craft could be launched at any moment now, and armed the Lintoo's weaponry in preparation for an attack. As soon as Vinta arrived at the pilot's station, he told her to take the weapons seat and start monitoring for Amburan craft. He hoped she remembered the training she had had at the Sector Combat School.

At altitude, he entered the coordinates for the colony site and instantly touched the course engagement icon. Just as he did, he heard Vinta shout.

"They're up!! Thanner they're up!!"

Thanner began manually descending at a rate of speed much beyond the range of safety. He'd have to guess when to disengage the downward force field. If he did it too late, the Lintoo would slam into the Earth at a rate of speed that would disintegrate the huge vessel in a gigantic explosion. On the screen, he saw the ground coming closer and closer. Vinta swung around in her chair and fixed her eyes on the vision of the fast-approaching Earth. She couldn't watch, and closed her eyes then grabbed the arms of her chair, preparing for the impact. Thanner suddenly touched the disengagement icon. He, too, was readying himself for the cataclysmic collision. He clenched his jaws. The screen showed the Lintoo had stopped no more than one hundred feet from the surface. Thanner put his finger on the manual screen and quickly lowered the Lintoo onto the ground then immediately turned off all power on the Lintoo to avoid heat detection. Vinta opened her eyes and saw the jungle on the outside screen. Her head dropped back onto the top of her chair. She closed her eyes and whispered a prayer of thanks. Raising her head, she looked at Thanner. His face showed an intense expression of suspense. She realized that he was waiting to see if they had been detected by the Amburans. With the power off, they had no way of knowing the whereabouts of the Amburan search force. Thanner suddenly jumped up and ran from the pilot station. Vinta followed him. He ran the long corridor to the exit area and turned the manual valve that allowed the ramp to drop down to the ground by gravity. As soon as it was down they both ran to the bottom and began scanning the sky for any sign of Amburans. He knew they would be cloaked and thus invisible, but would become visible if they descended toward the ground.

As he watched, he wasn't sure why he was doing so. If they were detected, the story was over. An Amburan attack force would assemble and would vaporize the Lintoo and everyone in it or anywhere near it. Then they would land to search for anyone who may have taken to the jungle to hide. Realizing there was nothing they could do but to wait to see if they were going to be instantly killed by a neutron blast, Thanner sat on the ground and leaned against a tree. Vinta sat beside him. They were silent. There was nothing to say. Any moment could be their last. Vinta reached over and took Thanner's hand. If she was to die, she wanted to do so holding the hand of the man she loved. She smiled at Thanner and he returned it ... then leaned his head against the tree and closed his eyes. Vinta leaned her head on his shoulder.

As they sat there, the Earthlings began to cautiously appear at the top of the ramp then, tentatively, made their way down to the jungle floor. They all knew their lives were hanging by a slenderest of threads and that each breath could be their last. Eventually, the entire group was seated on the ground in almost reverent silence, awaiting their fate. Occasionally heads would glance upward ... hopeful and fearful. As the night wore on, many fell asleep, particularly the children. The sky began hinting at the promise of a new day, appearing in its grey cloak then abruptly transforming itself into fresh and joyful blue. The awakening crowd looked at one another in cautious optimism ... prudently restraining yearning smiles.

Thanner awakened Vinta as he tried to gently lower her head to the ground before he stood up. She looked at him with fear in her eyes and then realized that the dawn was a proclamation that they had survived the night. She formed her face into a question ... to which Thanner shrugged in ambivalence. Others were also getting to their feet. Quiet conversation began to emerge, and the voyagers moved toward the large ramp and into the Lintoo ... seeking the comfort of their temporary home. Vinta guided them to the sleeping quarters where each family chose their room, among the thousand available. They stowed the clothes they had brought with them and put their toiletries in the proper places in the bathrooms. The showering process began, and an hour later, all reappeared in the huge lounge area with freshly washed hair and bodies, brushed teeth, glowing with the renewed spirit that comes with it. Appetites were raging and Vinta showed them to the dining area then conducted a primer on the use of Amburan cooking devices. Breakfast was prepared, including freshly brewed coffee.

Before they began eating, Tyler McFarland stood on a chair at the front of the immense dining room and addressed the crowd.

"I know we're all starved, but something needs to be said here. I'm not a speechmaker, but I'm going to try. Thanner and Vinta won't know what I'm talking about ... but we are Pilgrims here ... and this is our First Thanksgiving. We give thanks to God for being delivered from death by our Amburan friends. Thanner and Vinta risked their lives to save us and our children – those born and to be born. They've given us a chance to start over in a new land ... just like our forefathers. We will face difficulties and we may not make it ... but at least we have a chance at a new life. I thank God for giving us Thanner and Vinta and keeping us safe from those who wanted to kill us."

Tyler looked down at Annie holding Cassie tightly in her arms. Tears began to roll down his cheeks. Seeing this, many joined him in sharing tears of joy – including Vinta

Zuly. She stood up, walked to Tyler, and embraced him ... their heads being on the same plane with him on the chair. Vinta turned toward the group and spoke to them.

"I'm not sure of your customs on Earth in speaking to God ... but regardless, we speak to the same God of the universe. Through the centuries, many Sectors tried to proclaim our God to be dead ... but our God wasn't swayed by the petty grumblings of silly, arrogant creatures. He lives as he always has and always will. Our God is our Mother and Father who gave us life and who love us always ... and who will welcome us with open arms when we leave this plane of existence at the time of our death. In our Sector, we raise our arms and faces to God when we talk to him."

Vinta raised her arms and her face upward. The audience joined her.

"Our dear Mother and Father. We love you, and we thank you for being near us in all times of joy, fear, and sorrow ... and guiding us when we are lost. We ask you to protect us against those who wish to do us harm. If you can, please touch their hearts and help them understand that what they are doing is harming your innocent children. Please give us the wisdom and strength to survive and prosper in this, our new home. Bless us and keep us in your protective hands and comfort us in the trying times we will face. Amen."

An "Amen" resonated from the inspired Pilgrims. They ate their First Thanksgiving meal with hearts filled with hope and profound gratitude.